THE GRANT BROTHERS SERIES BOOK 5

KATHI S. BARTON

This is a work of fiction. Names, characters, places, and incidents are products of the author's imagination or are used factiously and are not to be construed as real. Any resemblance to actual events, locations, organizations, or person, living or dead, is entirely coincidental.

WCP

World Castle Publishing
Pensacola, Florida

Copyright © by Kathi S. Barton 2011
ISBN: 9781937593490
First Edition World Castle Publishing December 20, 2011
http://www.worldcastlepublishing.com

License Notes

Cover: Karen Fuller
Photo used on cover from Shutterstock
Editor: Brieanna Robertson

Chapter 1

Dane Wallace watched the man walk by her and released the breath she had been holding. He was safe for another night. Picking up her bag, she made her way to her car parked on High Street. She was nearly home before she let herself think what she was doing. Again.

For the past three nights she had been going to sit on the park bench at dusk to watch this stranger walk by her. Dane knew if he noticed her he would probably not come this way again, and she was sort of hoping for that. But the dream had not changed in the two weeks before she started coming here and it had not changed in the three nights since. Her cell phone rang when she was stopped at a light. She groaned when she read the caller ID.

"Hello, Pi. I'm on my way home now. Why don't you order us a pizza and I'll pick it up for us?"

"Missy Dane, you get hurt and I not have a house to pee in. You should tell police. Not walk streets like common hooker."

Pi and Dane had been living together for ten years and she still could not get the idioms right. Dane hardly noticed it anymore.

"I'm fine. Just order the pizza and I'll pick it up. I'll even bring you home some cola if you promise not to nag me anymore tonight."

"You bring home what I order? What if I order fishy pieces and eggs? You eat then?"

"If you order anything fishy on my half I'll send you back to China on a slow boat with all women. Tell me where you're ordering from and call. I'm tired and I have a headache."

"You be dead if you don't get help. I order from the Daddy place. You like him. He has nice commercials too. I want root beer, not cola. I like bubbles."

"I'll be home in an hour. Make sure you tell them I'll pick it up in forty minutes. And order a large salad and bread sticks. I have class tomorrow and I can take it for lunch."

After they hung up, Dane thought about Pi and their strange but strong bond. Even after ten years, Dane barely knew much more than Pi's last name and the only thing personal she knew about the older woman was what she had read in her file and the tiny snippets she'd gotten from touching her. Dane had gone to her country for a seminar and to learn the culture at sixteen. She then ended up trying to help find Pi's daughter.

Ping Chang had been walking home from college one day and had simply disappeared. Dane had been called in to help. Her special talents were revered rather than ridiculed in that country like they had been in the States and when asked, Dane had tried her very best to find the then eighteen-year-old girl. Dane knew that the girl was troubled, but she didn't know the extent of it until it was too late.

It had only taken her four days to find the girl. Her body had been in a boat that was sitting in a harbor. Ping had committed suicide. She had shamed her family by unknowingly having an affair with a married man and had gotten pregnant. Dane told Pi this after she told the police where Ping was.

"She was heartbroken and when she wrote the letter, she...she was most upset that she couldn't come to you."

"Why, Missy Dane? Why she not come to Momma? I love her. She my only baby. Why, Missy Dane?"

Dane didn't have answers for Pi, but she did have friendship to offer. When Dane had gone back to the States after her education, and then suddenly returned several months later, Pi had opened her home and her heart to the then broken Dane.

Dane had changed a great deal in the ten years. When she had come back to China after an incident in Chicago, she was badly injured and had lost a great deal of weight. Now she was a very beautiful woman. She also had a better sense of her self-worth and her abilities. Now Dane could help most of the time and it didn't hurt her as it had before.

Her hair was a plethora of autumn colors, browns, reds, yellows, and even some deep black that looked almost blue. Her olive complexion was light, but come summer she would tan nicely and become a golden brown. The sprinkle of freckles over her nose and shoulders gave her the appearance of someone very young, she knew this. But she also knew she had a body that left no doubt that she was very much a mature woman. Her full breasts were large, much larger than someone with her tall, slim frame would be able to carry off, she supposed. But she thought she wore them very well. Her dark green eyes sparkled. She supposed she looked okay, but never really cared one way or the other.

After picking up the pizza without anchovies, salad, and bread sticks and heading home, Dane thought about the man on the campus. She didn't know anything about him other than she must have touched him somewhere over their lifetimes. It would only take a small bump, an accidental touch of skin to skin. It was so dark where she had to wait for him to pass her, she wasn't even sure what he looked like. But she knew that if she didn't intervene, he would die. And if he did, it would be her fault.

It was seven o'clock in the morning before Dane decided to go to bed. She had finished up her reports due the following week and had made a list of things she was going to do this weekend. The emails she had put off until the very last minute and even now, put it off for another day. They would still be there tomorrow. There was nothing ever in it that couldn't wait. She was brushing her teeth and getting ready to get into bed when she stormed back into the office and looked through them. Nothing. But she knew that if she hadn't checked, she would only toss and turn until she did.

Pi woke her at noon to tell her there was a phone call for her. "Man say to tell you it important. Said that you are only one to help. I tell him you no help without sleep and he told me to wake you."

"Tell him I'll be right there." Dane dumped herself out of the bed and sat on the floor for a couple of minutes before she got up and pulled on her robe. She knew it could only be one person. He was the only one with this phone number. Picking up the receiver in the office, she snarled at him.

"I get four hours of sleep every day. You couldn't wait until two or later to call and bug the shit out of me? It's barely nine o'clock where you are. This had better be important."

"Dane, I have another one for you."

Before she could catch herself, Dane was on the floor again. The room had tilted and she couldn't keep up with the way the room shifted and dropped. Her head was spinning and she could just make out someone yelling her name.

"You make her sick again, I put hex on your cock. It never work again. I told you before no more. Why you tell her stuff that make her sick? I will do it you—"

"Pi, give me the phone. It's all right. He needs me and he's the only one I trust. Let me have the phone and could you please fix me a glass of tea?"

Dane didn't think she was going to do it, and before she handed Dane the phone, she told Markus once more about the hex. Dane didn't think Pi knew how to spell hex much less try to execute one, but didn't think now was a good time to point that out.

"Tell me as much as you can. I'm not quite settled just yet, but I do have an office downtown. I don't know...I think I need a break soon, Markus. This is taking more out of me all the time without any down time. I told you before how much it takes from me."

"I told them that. Jefferies said to tell you he has your back. I told him I was doing just fine with it, but thanks. I also, well, I told him you wouldn't come and he offered five times your fee. I said I'd ask. Dane, I can't do this without you. But I can understand why...this little boy. They think it's...I know you don't want information, but it's been four days. You know as well as I do what the chances of getting them back even after twenty-four hours are. They didn't let me know until this morning."

"Send me what you have. Right now I can't leave here. There's something going on where I am. Don't give Jefferies anything until I call you after I receive the information. Markus, make sure you send the usual with the paperwork too."

"Got it. You should have it before ten tomorrow morning. Will Pi...I know she hates me, but will she accept the package if it comes before you're awake?"

Dane didn't know, but thought there was a good chance she wouldn't. Pi hated Markus and it was nothing he'd done so much as what had happened to her. Dane took a deep breath and closed her eyes. "You just send it and I'll make sure she signs for it."

It took Dane two hours and a promise of a day at the spa for Pi to agree to accept the package from Markus. By the time Dane was getting out of the shower to go to work, she had the makings of a major headache. Pulling on the first thing she could grab, she was ten minutes behind and had forgotten her lunch.

~~~

"Jamie, please come over for dinner? We haven't seen you since we got back from our honeymoon. I miss you. I'll have Byron make your favorite meal?"

Jamie had to smile. Byron had married Jamie's best friend and his brother did all the cooking. Of course Taylor did most everything else, but cooking was not something she even was sort of okay at. Taylor was, by far, a worse cook than even his and Byron's mother. And that was saying a lot.

"All right, but I have a late class tonight so I won't be able to come over until after six. And I want pasta alfredo with chicken. And apple pie for dessert. Tell him not the store bought kind either. I want him cutting up apples and making crust. Tell him if he wears an apron all night, I won't tell you about the time he was caught with Beth in the back seat of Mom's car."

"Ah, you mean the girl he popped his cherry with? Yeah, he told me about that. He also told me about the time you two were caught in his bedroom with Sadie and Angel Davison. Shame on you, James Grant! That poor girl is probably scarred for life."

Jamie sat up in his chair and was ready to blast his brother when his other line rang. "It was her fault. I'd never had anyone...you know, I'm not going to justify this to you. Suffice it to say, she is not scarred. I gotta go, I'll see you tonight. Love ya, Ta." Jamie cut his friend off while she was still laughing. "James Grant."

"What a way to answer your phone. Does anyone say, 'Hello, Mother, how was your day?' anymore. I was wondering if you've heard from your brother yet? He is supposed to be at the house this weekend and I don't know what he wants for his birthday dinner. And are you bringing a date? A mother likes to know these things."

Jamie had to smile at his mother. There was no doubt in his mind that she was the most loved mother in the world and she had each of her sons, including their wives, wrapped tightly around her fingers. And he knew this was her way of reminding them all that it was Byron's birthday this weekend. He could get a date, but he was not really seeing anyone he wanted to take to his family's house. That was something no man did to a causal date. The girl did fine, but the man would hear about it for months.

James Grant had no delusions about his looks. He knew he was pretty good-looking, or so women had been telling him since he knew the difference between boys and girls, he thought with a grin. He was well over six feet tall and had a head full of black hair. It was longer than his brothers', just over his collar and while not curly, it had a wave to it that women could not resist touching. His body was tight with muscle and not the kind made in a gym, but of hard work and real labor. Every year he and one of his brothers or more would be at a project site somewhere building a house for some organization. He also helped the elderly with construction projects they needed around their house in his free time. His hard jaw was in direct contrast to his easy nature, he knew. His mother often told him that he had a hard head, too, but he doubted it was a compliment. Dark brown eyes and long thick lashes under dark brows gave him his rugged looks, and his high cheek bones and sloped nose hinted of his Indian heritage back along his family line. Jamie, to his friends and family, was hard to anger and quick to forgive. He'd always tried to live by that.

"I'm going over to have dinner with them tonight as a matter of fact. Taylor is cooking me my favorite dinner. And apple pie for dessert." He waited for the explosion and was not disappointed.

"Oh good heavens! Please tell me she's not cooking again. I don't think I've ever had anyone burn a cup of coffee before. Oh, Jamie, take over some pizza or something. Don't let her poison you. I love the girl very much, but...you're kidding me, aren't you?"

"Yes, Mom, I am. Byron is cooking. But he is making me my favorite. I have a late meeting then I'm going over there at six. You should come with me. I'm sure they won't mind." He was positive they would not mind, but hoped for some reason she said no. He loved spending time with his brother and Ta.

"No, I have two meetings as well. I also have to go over and see to this family. Why some people think it's their right to abuse children...I'll talk to you tomorrow. Tell them I love them and will see them both on Sunday."

After hanging up, Jamie made a few calls and started over to the lecture hall to begin his class. He almost drove over, but it was such a lovely evening that he walked. It took him a little longer because he kept getting distracted by the girls—women really, who were out on the Quad sun bathing.

The campus at Ohio State was huge. It spread out over a massive amount of space, but there were buses every ten minutes or so to get you from one point to the other in no time. He was still headed to the meeting when he felt an odd sort of tingle.

He slowed his pace a little and started just looking around when he noticed a man and a woman staring at him. Well, staring was a strong term, he thought, but they were looking his way very intently. When he started to look back more, they suddenly turned and walked in the opposite direction. The hair on the back of his neck stood up and he tried to remember everything he could about them. When his watch beeped to tell him he was running late, he took off at a gentle lope and made it just as the meeting was being called to order. Before he started taking notes, however, he make a list of everything he remembered about the couple and thought his sister-in-law Cait, a detective, would be proud of him.

$\mathcal{C}hapter\ 2$

Dane was just sitting down when her cell phone went off. She looked at the caller ID and moaned. Not now. She liked sitting quietly and waiting for the man to come by, not talking on the phone. Before she could decide if she was going to answer, she felt a stir in the air. He was coming. Tonight was going to be the night, she just knew it.

Sitting back further on the bench, she tried to concentrate on the area around her. She could feel...not anger, but something more. Hatred, violent hatred, too. She could not tell where it was coming from, but she could tell that it was close. Much closer than the man was. She thought about the dream and shuddered.

In the dream, he was walking by the bench and someone came out of the shadows and threw him to the ground. He fought hard, but when the second person came out and stabbed him in the chest, he began to lose the fight. Getting weaker, the two attackers started to push harder at killing him. Because that was their intent; the man was to die. He bled to death before he was found several hours later. Dane couldn't, no, she wouldn't let that happen again.

The man's closeness moved over her. His calm mind and easy thoughts were soothing to her. Dane reached out and tried to center on his thoughts, but like what happens most of the time; they are too many and too jumbled to get any single one. It wasn't easy to read the mind of someone with obvious intellect. Suddenly, he was in front of her and as he took two steps beyond her, she thought that she was wrong tonight again and sighed.

The attacker sprung forward so quickly Dane was too startled to react for several seconds. Then when the younger man started to moan, she jumped up and kicked his assailant in the ribs and off the young man. She didn't know who looked more surprised by her kick, the attacker or the young man.

Before the victim could get up and help, the second attacker hit Dane in the back with something. She tumbled to the ground and landed over her man. Attacker one kicked her in the head and soon Dane was seeing stars, but had no time to appreciate the pretty colors when attacker two grabbed her by the hair and jerked her up. Just as the fist was coming back to hit Dane, Dane lifted her booted foot and kicked her in the kneecap, bending it backwards with a loud snap. The scream was loud in the otherwise quiet area. She released Dane immediately, but she was not able to keep standing. Another blow to Dane's head made her dizzy and she dropped to the ground. The man Dane was there to help, the hapless victim, hit attacker once again and he took off, leaving his partner unconscious on the ground beside Dane. Her last thought before she slipped into her own unconscious state was that the young man was damned good-looking.

"Dr. Wallace? Dr. Wallace, can you hear me?" Dane opened her eyes and tried to focus on the girl in front of her. It was too much effort and she closed them again. "Dr. Wallace, I need for you to look at me. I have to ask you a few questions."

"You're not supposed to tell me my name, first of all, and secondly, I can hear you fine. It's my head that hurts, not my ears. Where am I?" Dane tried to sit up, but the pain was too much.

"University Hospital. They brought you in about thirty minutes ago. Can you tell me the date?"

"It was five o'clock when I went to the Quad and since it's probably still the same date, I'll assume it's April twenty-fourth. I haven't really kept up on the political part of the States yet so don't ask me the president. I might know it, but my head hurts too much to try and figure it out right now."

"Dr. Sheppard will be in to see you soon." Humor laced the nurse's voice. "Are you hurting anywhere else but your head? Mr. Grant said that he thought you might have been hit in the back as well."

"Mr. Grant?" Her head was still fuzzy, but the name Grant meant nothing to her. She gave up trying to concentrate on just working through the pain; there were too many other emotions in the room for her to do that. Dane closed her eyes and concentrated on building a wall around her to block out the bombardment of feelings hitting her. This was why she avoided crowds of people and especially hospitals.

"He's the man you saved. His family is with him now. I think Dr. Sheppard is releasing him soon." The curtain moved and Dane heard clicking, then the nurse continued. "But he's not releasing you, though."

Releasing him soon meant that he was all right. Dane relaxed for a few minutes and thought, one more. She'd been able to help one more. There had been a time when she decided that she'd had enough. That's when she'd moved — no, escaped would be a better term — to China. She'd been betrayed by the very people she'd been trying to help.

17

"Dr. Wallace? My name is Alex Sheppard. I'm the on duty emergency room doctor. I've gotten your x-rays back and there doesn't seem to be any cracks in your skull, but I would like to keep you over night. You were out for over thirty minutes and that has me concerned. If you'll lean up, I'd like to have a look at your back as well. Jamie said that you were hit with a piece of wood and he was surprised you didn't complain about it more."

"I didn't complain at all. Seems this Jamie person was more aware than me. Maybe I should have just let him take care of them himself. My back is fine. My head, however, feels like a freight train has gone—"

"Missy Dane! Missy Dane, where you be?"

"Holy Christ, you called Pi. You can't tell her anything. She is...well, I was going to say slightly over protective, but that's like saying I'm slightly a woman. Just play down everything, all right?"

Alex was nodding when the curtain flew back and Pi was grabbing her. For a tiny woman, she could hug tighter than anyone Dane knew. And since she was speaking in Chinese, Dane answered her the same way.

"I'm fine, I swear. I just slipped and hit my head on the bench. Nothing happened that you should be this worked up about. How did you find out anyway?"

"You didn't call. I worry for you. You didn't call. Then news person say two people mugged on campus, I knew it you. I told you, I told you to call police. But you never listen." Pi hugged her again. "What I do without you?"

"I'm fine, Pi, I promise. They're just going to keep me over night to make—"

"Over night? No, Pi will stay too. You not be alone. I stay too. You scare me. Never do that again, Missy Dane."

The doctor had left at some point and Pi had crawled up into her bed. Now that someone had pointed it out, her back was killing her. Dane bit her lip and kept quiet. Pi was already upset and there was no reason to make it worse. The nurse came in a few minutes later and said that she was going to transfer Dane to the third floor.

"Pi, you have to go home and bring me back some clothes and some personal items in an overnight case. And you can't stay all night. I need you to sign for that package tomorrow. I'm sorry. But you can call me whenever you want."

"No, Missy Dane. I stay. No package worth something happen to you. I will keep you safe." There was a noise at the front of the curtain. Dane looked up in time to see her past slam into her.

~~~

Cait stared at the two women on the bed and it took her several seconds to realize who they were. Well, at least who the younger woman was. Christ, there had to be a mistake. She glanced up at the piece of tape over the bed and realized it was not a mistake. Dane Messenger had moved back to the States.

Neither of them moved until the oriental woman squeaked. "You hurt me, Missy Dane. Let go my arm. I go to get stuff."

"No!" Dane shouted to her. "I'm not staying. Go and get the nurse and tell her I've changed my mind. I'm all right and I'm leaving."

"Missy Dane, you think —"

"Now, Pi. Go get the nurse." Cait watched at Dane threw off the sheet and was beginning to stand. The older woman moved out of the curtained area, but she kept looking back at Dane and Cait. Before Cait could speak, Spencer and Jamie came around the curtain too.

19

"You found her, good. I was wondering where you'd gone off to. So this is the woman who saved my brother's life. I'm Spencer Grant. And you would be...?"

"Leaving." Dane grabbed the bed when she stood, dizziness overwhelming her for a moment. "I'm glad you're all right, Mr. Grant, but I've just remembered I have somewhere else to be. And if you all don't mind, I'd like to change."

"Dane, please don't go. I'm not here under any official business. I'm just—" Cait started to say.

"Frankly, Detective O'Malley, I don't give two good shits why you're here. You just are. I'm leaving and if you try and contact me, I swear to you that I'll sue you so fast your head will spin. Either you leave or I dress in front of you. Your choice."

No one moved. Cait knew she would do it and was not surprised when Dane shrugged and pulled the gown up over her head. Luckily, her back was to them, or unluckily. When she took off her shirt, it gave them all a view of her bare, scarred, and bruised back. Cait had seen her back before, but there had been open wounds back then. The bruise was new.

"Holy Mother of God. Who did that to you?" Jamie cried out just as Spencer moved forward.

It was too late to stop him. He touched Dane on the shoulders with both his bare hands and Dane screamed. Dropping to the floor, she screamed again as her body jerked and convulsed. Cait rushed to her husband and pulled him away from her. But the damage was done.

"Get out. All of you get out and leave me alone. I beg you, please get out." Dane tried to stand, but staggered, and when she moved to hold on to the bed, Cait moved her brother-in-law and husband out and called for Damon to come quick. Most of the staff in the emergency department had come running when Dane screamed. Cait moved back beside Dane, careful not to touch her, and told everyone but Damon to get out.

"Damon, help her up, but don't touch her skin. Wrap her gown around her shoulders if you have to, but don't touch her. Jamie, I said to—"

"I'm not leaving. What can I do to help?" Cait looked at the woman still huddled on the floor and wished that she knew. "Don't touch her."

"Yeah, I got that part. Are you going to let my brother take a look at your back, miss? He's a good doctor, one of the best." Cait looked at Jamie and wondered at his anger, but didn't comment.

"No. I want you all to get out. And take her with you. I'm leaving as soon as my friend gets back." Dane was standing now, not very well, but she was off the floor and had her gown over her breasts.

Cait reached under the bed and pulled out the bag that the staff had put her clothes in when Dane was brought in. Cait dumped the contents on the bed and picked up the shirt.

"I wouldn't put the bra back on, not with that injury. If you need help with changing, I can get you a nurse. I do need to get a statement from you about what happened. I know you don't like me, but—"

"I loathe you. I'll give my statement to anyone but you. Not that I figure anyone connected to you will get it right, but I'll give it to them."

"Now see here, that's no way to talk to my wife. I'll have—"

"Wife? Christ, could this get any more surreal? And this man, he's your brother-in-law? I don't believe it. You know, on second thought, I don't remember a damned thing that happened. I just remember waking up here and nothing more. I guess you'll have to—"

"Dane, that's enough," Cait finally snapped. "My family didn't have anything to do with what happened between you and me. Let Damon look at your back and I'll take your statement. Once we're through, you can leave."

Cait was not sure she was going to cooperate, but after several tense seconds, she turned so that Damon could examine her back. It did not get any better with a second look.

The board, or whatever they had used to hit her with, had caught her right across the middle of her back. It was already darkening and there were a couple of abrasions. Damon lifted his hands several times, but he did not touch her.

"If you let me know when you're going to touch me, I'll be able to brace for it. It's the sudden unexpected that hurts. Try not to linger. I'll let you know when you need to step back." Dane's voice was low and tight.

Cait watched as Damon spoke softly to Dane and watched as she tensed up under his touch. Dane must have learned a great of deal control in the ten years since she had seen her. Before, she hadn't been able to have anyone touch her for any amount of time. Jamie went to stand in front of Dane and smiled encouragingly.

"If I use your gown, can I have you brace against me? Sometimes it helps to have something to push against when he checks for broken ribs. I've had a few broken in my time."

"No. I can...it'll be too much. I can't...there are too many...no. I'll be fine. Thank you."

Cait stepped out of the curtained area and into Spencer's arms. She hated to cry, but no one had ever told her that they loathed her before. Nor did she feel she did not deserve it.

She had done Dane wrong and she had every reason in the world to hate her as much as she did.

"O'Malley, honey. Tell me what happened in there. What's the history between the two of you?" He stroked her belly, huge now with their child.

"I can't. Not until I...she has good reason to hate me, Grant. I hurt her. And I'm part of the reason she's scarred like she is, both on her back and in her soul."

Chapter 3

Pi showed up a few minutes into the exam, but luckily, she was waylaid by Cait so she didn't see Dane's back. When Damon finished and Jamie stepped out, Dane pulled her shirt over her head and waited. She didn't have long.

"I wish you'd reconsider spending the night, Miss Wallace." Damon was pulling off his gloves as he spoke. "The injury to your head it quite severe and your back is badly bruised. We can keep an eye on you in the event that something happens through the night."

"It's doctor, and no. I'm going home. I think I've had enough excitement for one night. Thanks for your concern, but I think I'll take my chances at home. If you could have someone give me the proper paperwork to sign, I'll be ready to go."

"A doctor of what, if you don't mind me asking?" Damon sat on the bed and looked like he didn't have a care in the world. Probably didn't.

"Psychology, I'm a Psychologist. I deal with children who have had trauma in their lives. I take a few adults, but not many. I'm…I'm waiting on my boards to come through. I've not been in the States for a while."

"Where are you going to practice? I'm always looking for someone to help with children that have a lot to deal with. It seems that they have more and more to deal with all the time."

She didn't answer. She supposed he could find her if he wanted, or at least her office. But she didn't want to get friendly with these people. That would mean dealing with Cait O'Malley, well, Grant, she supposed.

"Are you telepath or empathic, Doctor Wallace? The reason I can guess that is because of the issue with being touched. I thought at first it was from the beating you took, but that's not it. Or at least not all of it. Your not wanting people to touch your bare skin is because you can feel much more that way, I'm guessing."

She looked at him and her respect for his intelligence rose significantly. But she still didn't trust him. She continued to get dressed, not saying a word.

She was both and more, actually. Both a telepath and an empath with a healthy dose of clairvoyance too. He was right about the touching too. Bare skin touching sent her over the edge; the feelings and thoughts of the other person would bombarded her so hard and fast she would have a migraine for days. It was bad enough being in the hospital with all the despair and pain, but having someone touch her would make her hurt so badly that it would be days before she could sort through all the emotions and feelings to know much about the person.

"Dr. Grant, tell your brother, the one who touched me, that his child will be fine. So will Detective O'Malley. He...I saw them holding him, the baby. I...please don't tell anyone."

"No. No, I won't. Thank you. If you have any problems, I'd like for you to call me. Here's my home number and my cell. I won't tell anyone. I realize that telling you that you can trust me is a little farfetched, but you can. I won't betray your trust." She hesitated before taking the card he held out to her, but she put it into her back pocket without a word. She was sure she'd never call it, but took it anyway.

"We'll see, I guess." Pi came around the curtain as Dane was tying her shoe, the nurse right behind her. After signing the paper work, Dane remembered the statement. "Shit. I have to talk to the police."

"Go ahead on home. I'll take care of Cait. If you'll promise to call the station when you get up in the morning, I'll let Cait know."

"Missy Dane sleep only few hours then she up all night. She call station house after one. I make her remember. You go away now, we go home. Shoo!" Dane laughed at the expression on Damon's face and went out into the early morning with Pi beside her. The cab was waiting for them.

The cab dropped them off at the mall and they took a bus to the station. From there they took another cab to the hospital again then they walked home. Neither of them said a word on the ride other than to tell the driver where they were going. Dane never took the direct route home, not when it was easier to take the long way round. Pi was used to the way her mistress did things and rarely commented anymore. Besides, if Pi wanted home sooner, she didn't have to stay with Dane. It was almost four in the morning when they unlocked the front door to the house. Pi went to bed, Dane to her office.

It had been almost ten years since she'd seen Cait. Officer O'Malley, as she had been then, and her Captain Hunter had been a part of the task force that was searching for a serial killer. Dane reached into her desk and pulled out the worn file. Taking a deep breath, she opened it.

The headlines were the first thing there. "Seven Dead and No End in Sight." The next was more gruesome. "Ten Dead Girls and Not a Clue." Dane picked up two of the pictures.

The first one was of a little girl, Danielle Sams. She had been the fifth victim. She would have been about twenty now had she lived. She had been brutally murdered and then her body had been torn apart. They had found seventy-three stab wounds over her little torso and more along her arms and legs. She had not been raped, thank goodness, but she had been made to suffer. She had been gone five days when she was found.

The next picture was of Shelby Thomas. Shelby had been five at the time of her murder and she was the ninth. The murders were nearly the same except that Shelby had had her head removed. It had been done before she had died. Dane stared at the body and wondered again, even after all these years, hadn't anyone else noticed that the little girl had a name written in blood on her along her thigh. It was the first thing Dane had noticed when she went to the police station to offer her help.

At first they acted like she'd had something to do with it. Then later, when she'd told them what she could to, they treated her like she was insane. She had explained to Hunter that she had been finding missing people for years and had in fact just gotten back from China where she had helped find another missing girl. He just laughed at her.

Dane knew better than to go directly to the parents of the victims. She had learned the hard way that police didn't like people like her "fucking" with their case. So she'd had her mother do it.

Shannon Messenger had not wanted to be associated with her freakish daughter's silly notions, but when Dane's grandmother stepped in, Shannon asked the two families to meet at her house. Dane had asked that they bring something of their child's with them. If her mother would have believed in her, or Dane had just kept her mouth shut, or any one hundred other things that she could have, should have or maybe if's she had done, Dane would have been fine.

The parents of Shelby had come. The parents of Danielle declined. Dane explained what she was going to do and waited for them to ask questions. At sixteen, Dane could not believe that anyone would think she was doing anything but trying to help them. But then, she had grown up a lot since then. She picked up Shelby's shirt, held it in her hands, and closed her eyes.

"There are two, no, three men. They are tall, one is dark the other two are light, thinner than the first. Shelby was not afraid of the darker man. She knows him, he's…he's close. She had a teddy bear, one the dark man gave her to get her to go with him. It's a van, white or tan. The plate number is seven eight three then I think 'm' or 'n,' 'w' and 'p.' They're not Illinois plates. These are lighter, the background is colorful. Shelby is picked up at the bus stop and he tells her that her mother…no, her grandmother is waiting for her. He tells her that her mommy and daddy have been hurt. She gets in with him. One of the lighter men, younger than either of the other two, puts a bag over her head and smothers her. She is dismembered later at a garage. There are buses. They aren't school buses but I think tour ones. They're too nice for city ones. There's a street sign, Mac…Mac something, I can't make it out."

Dane opened her eyes and looked at the couple. Shock and disbelief were evident on their faces. Before Dane could say anything, her mother stood up.

"You horrible child." And the slap was swift and painful. "If I'd known what you were going to say to these lovely people, I would never have done what you asked me to. You'll have to forgive me, my daughter is somewhat of trouble maker. She's been so her entire life. I'm just sorry you had to be witness to my humiliation."

"I'm not lying. That's what happened." The slap came again, this time knocking her off the couch. Dane sat there and held her cheek as her mother rushed the couple out of the house. Before she returned, Dane went to her room.

For two days, Dane had to listen to her mother wail about what Dane had done. How she had humiliated the family name and that no one would want anything to do with them again. Two days of being locked in her room with nothing more to eat than a slice of bread slid under the door by one of the maids and sometimes a candy bar. On the night of the third day, Dane climbed out her second story window and went to find the warehouse. With her computer, she had searched for each of the bus garages in the area and had the name of four. She was determined to find enough evidence to take to the police. She found what she needed on the second try.

~~~

Jamie sat in the kitchen of his brother's home and looked at his sister-in-law. He had no doubt what she was telling him was something she believed, but he didn't. Mind readers just did not exist.

"She took me to the bus garage and showed me just where the girl had been cut up. She said that three of the ten girls had been murdered there, but five had been cut up in the garage. I didn't believe her either. I wish I had. Captain Hunter told me to file her information in the circular file cabinet and to move on to the real work. I did, I'm sorry to say. I was green. She was a kid, even if she was only a few years younger than me. But she didn't stop. Three days later,

Dane called me again. She had them in the garage and she had a gun on them. They had…the men had kidnapped another child, the twelfth, and they had already murdered her. Dane had left me three messages and I never got them. Hunter had had them thrown away."

"How did she catch them? I mean, damn, sixteen and holding a gun on three grown men? Her parents must have had a change of heart." When Cait got up and moved to the kitchen window, Jamie knew he would not like this.

"She followed them for three days until they took another child. If I had gotten the first message, we may have been able to save Allison. The second maybe, too, but by the third, she was already dead.

"By the time I showed up, Dane had already tried to save Allison and had a gun pointed at the three men. She was so angry, so very angry, that I couldn't look at her. When Captain Hunter showed up, he had her put in the back of a cruiser and taken away. I thought to the hospital. She'd had a few bruises on her face. He'd had her taken to her parents.

"The papers hailed the police as heroes. When I asked about Dane's involvement, he said that she was a minor and that her parents didn't want her name used. I understood it, but I thought she should be recognized in some way. I went by her house the next day and the butler told me that she was away for a while and that he would make sure she got the message. I went to work that night and there was a message from her parents and lawyer. Dane was being treated for her mental health issues and I was not to have any more contact with her or her family."

"You didn't stop, did you? You tried to find her. I bet that put her parents out of joint!" Jamie could just see Cait riding in and saving the young girl from all sorts of horrible treatments.

"The next night, a co-worker came in and said his wife had just been laid off. She was a bus driver for a privately owned line and that some rich bitch had come in tonight and told them they were all off until further notice. It wasn't until the next night that I found out who. Messenger Enterprises had purchased the line and had closed it down." Jamie watched Cait as she continued talking.

"The next morning when I got off work, I went by and saw three cars and a limo there. When they left a few hours later, there were four men and her mother, who entered the vehicles and left. I went inside to see what was going on. I...I found her. I found Dane.

"They had tied her up, naked, with her arms over her head and a gag in her mouth. She was...Christ, they had hung her over the blood that had been little Allison's and her feet were in the blood. I ran to her. I wanted to get her down, and that's when I saw what they'd done to her. Her back. They'd beaten her badly. The whip was still lying on the desk with her blood soaking it where they had laid it. I couldn't move. I didn't...I couldn't touch her so I called her grandmother who I'd met at the press conference. Within minutes, a private ambulance showed up and cut her down. They must have known. They never touched her without gloves. And the care they gave her was...it was my fault and Dane knew it. She was in and out of consciousness, talking and then screaming from the pain. She told me before they took her away that she would never forgive me, that I would rot in hell before...I don't know what happened to her after that. She disappeared. I tried to have her mother arrested, but everytime I got close to her, Hunter would yank me back. A few years later, I read where her mother had died. Her father had been out of the picture for a long time and there was no mention of Dane in the obituary. It said Shannon Messenger was childless."

"Her mother had her beaten?" Jamie asked, shocked. "What kind of sick monster has her own child beaten that badly? Then disowns her?"

"Dane's grandmother said that they were trying to beat the mental illness out of her. That wasn't the first time they had beaten Dane and if she hadn't disappeared, it more than likely wouldn't have been the last. Dane was brilliant, she said, and that she was fine where she was. That's all…that's all she would tell me and believe me, I asked a lot."

"How long did you keep tabs on her, baby?" Spencer asked. "And is her grandmother still alive?"

Jamie watched Cait as she sat back down in the chair easily, her pregnancy making it difficult to walk and sit well.

"No, her grandmother died six months ago. She had her attorney contact me and let me know. I never knew where Dane was, she'd never tell me, but I asked about her nearly every month until then."

"You believe she was there at the Quad because she knew I was going to get mugged, don't you?" Jamie shook his head. "You think that she somehow kept me from being mugged because of what she can supposedly do?"

"No, Jamie, I know she was there to save your life. If you were just being mugged, she wouldn't have been bothered by it. She knew that you were going to die and she had to save you."

Chapter 4

Dane woke at noon the next afternoon. There was a note from Pi telling that she'd gone to the grocery and that her package was in her office. She also said that Dane owed her two days at the spa. Dane smiled and got herself something to drink.

She was not ready to face the evidence just yet and sat at the table to drink her tea and eat a bowl of cereal. She was just finishing it when the phone rang. Without bothering to look at the ID, she answered it.

"I've had the night from hell. I've had the shit beat out of me with a two-by-four and the past has come up and bit me on the ass. I haven't had a chance to look at the evidence yet. You know I don't get up until after noon, so chill out. If you give me ten minutes, I'll call you back." There were several seconds of silence so long that Dane got up and looked at the caller ID. Local number, shit.

"This is Captain Tucker of the Columbus police department. I got this number from a car registration. Is this Danish Messenger?"

With a mumbled "fuck" under her breath, Dane answered, "Yes. This is Dane Messenger. I have a permit to park there over night, Captain. I was coming by to pick up my car today. Is there a problem?"

"No, ma'am, no problem." Dane didn't trust Captain Tucker's good ol' boy routine. "There was a mugging last night in the area and we were trying to find a car that might have belonged to one of the people involved. Yours was the one that no one could account for so we had to look into it. We've impounded the car, just to be on the safe side, so when you come in, you'll need to have some sort of an ID on you to claim it. There'll be no charge, of course, but like I said, we were just making sure."

"Sure. I understand." She wondered if he would say anything about her statement when she'd answered and closed her eyes, hoping he would not. It was too much to hope for, she supposed, when he did.

"I don't suppose that you want to tell me who beat the shit out of you with a two-by-four, would you? One of our vics last night was hit with something similar. Name's similar, but doesn't mean it can't be you, does it? And then I'd like to ask you about the evidence too. Miss Messenger, what are you doing in my fair city?"

"Nothing illegal, I assure you, and as such, none of your business. I'll go by the impound lot sometime today to get my car, Captain Tucker. If there's nothing else, I have things to do." His laughter brought her up short.

After getting the address, she sat down again and waited for Pi. Her head was pounding and her back felt as if someone had hit her with a board, lucky her. When Pi came in an hour later, Dane still had not looked at the evidence bag and she was still sitting in the kitchen. She couldn't deal with it just yet. She knew a boy's life was at stake, but if she didn't get a hold on her emotions then she wouldn't be able to help anyway.

After taking a cab to the impound lot and getting her car back, she drove to her office. She had taken the package with her and when she was finished with the last patients file, she closed and locked the door and opened the bags.

She did not pick up anything right away. She knew that even though they had used gloves to pick the items up and put them into the baggies, someone had to touch the outside some. It took Dane several minutes to clean the outsides with solvents. Nothing could remove the touches completely, but it could tone it down some. Taking off the gloves she'd used and picking up some scissors, she cut open the first bag. Taking a deep breath and closing her eyes, she picked up the first item.

Boy. Dog. Momma. Daddy. Hundreds of snippets of memories and touches passed in front of Dane's closed eyes. Thousands of scents, more of feelings — happiness, sadness, excitement, and sleep. Too much at first, then little by little, they slowed. More and more, she was able to sort them out, take them in. Nearly an hour after she picked up the sweater, she knew so much more about this little boy and his life than his parents or anyone would ever know. She also knew who had killed him. Opening the second baggie, she was flooded with the same emotions and touches, different people, different times, animals, and scents, but the same killer. Three hours after locking her office door, Dane called Markus.

~~~

Jamie was sitting in his office when the phone rang. He smiled. Someone from his family had been calling every hour since he'd left for work this morning. This was the second time his mom had called.

"I'm fine, Mom. I didn't get hurt and I will be more careful in the future." He heard her huff and he smiled bigger.

"See that you do. But that's not why I was calling. That girl, Dr. Wallace, I don't suppose you got her phone number, did you?"

"No. For some reason, I don't know why, but that didn't strike me as a date asking sort of situation. Besides, I don't think she's my type. I like my women to be much less bustier and more hips to grab onto." He could hear her sputtering and he laughed out loud.

"James Andrew Grant! Is that anyway to talk to your mother? Some days, I'm sure you were switched at birth. You are the only child of mine who would talk to me in such a way. What on earth is wrong with you?"

"Mom, you know I like my women tiny. Have you ever seen me date anyone that was bigger than a size 'b' cup? I mean, maybe Ta, but we never got beyond first base." He really was enjoying himself. And he and Taylor had never gotten past the kissing stage, too creepy. It was like kissing his sister.

"I'm hanging up now. I don't even know why I called, you have me so flustered. Shame on you, young man. I'll call you when I...bloody hell. There's been another child killed in California. The police are making a statement now."

Jamie reached over and turned on his television. It was never on anything but the news or the sports channel and now was no different. The special task force officer Markus Lionel was speaking.

"...this morning. He is also suspected in the murder of two other children who have not yet been located. We have a specialist that will be working with us on this case from this point on to try and ascertain where or if there are more. Any questions?"

"You say specialist. Is this the same man that helped on the Night Slasher several months ago? You said that he was instrumental in helping solve that case. My readers would really like to know who this man is."

"Sorry, April, but I have no comment on the specialist. I've told you before that we are working with a person who is helpful and is very private. Next question."

"Will the person be coming here to help with the location of the bodies? And if so, when do you expect him to arrive?"

"People, I have said all I'm going to say about the help. If there are no more questions about the man who murdered five children, then this is coming to a close. One more question, one more hint about the specialist, and it will be the last news conference I give. Do I make myself understood?"

Jamie watched the man walk away from the podium and head toward a closed door. At first he had thought of Dane then dismissed the idea as they asked about a man. But he could not get her helping them out of his mind. He remembered his mom was still on the phone.

"Mom, why did you need Dane's number, did you remember? I didn't get it, but she did talk to Damon a great deal. Maybe he has it."

"Yes. I already talked to him. That's how I knew to call her. I have a child that could benefit from her type of work. Did you know that she's a doctor? Anyway, I'll have to see if I can track her down another way. I love you, son. I'll see you on Sunday."

Jamie hung up and sat back again. Her name was Dane Wallace and she was new to the States, she'd said. He picked up the phone again and called Devin. He would be able to find her faster than anyone.

"I don't do date research anymore. You want to get to know a girl then you have to figure it out the old fashioned way. Through dating and talking. Why do you want this anyway?"

"Mom does. And I'm not dating her. We barely spoke two words to each other. Damon said she was a doctor. Mom needs her help. That's it."

"Oh. Well she has a practice on Thirty-fourth Street. It's only open in the late afternoon and evening. I can't find a home address for her, but I did find an application she is trying to get through on a Pi Lee Chang. She's a Chinese resident who wants to stay here on a working visa. Dane Wallace is the person who is asking for her help. They've been companions for nearly a decade in China. If Dane was a resident here before, I can't find it. There is no driver's license in her name, no social security number or anything else. The building is owned by some conglomerate that I can't seem to get a handle on. Everything seems legal, but who knows."

"You just happened to have that in front of you? Damn, Devin, you're better than I thought. Give me the address and I'll go see what I can find out. Who were you searching this for anyway?"

"She made O'Malley cry. I've never seen anyone do that before and I want to know how she did it. There's a history there that I can't figure out."

Jamie closed his eyes and wondered.

"Besides, I'm worried...I don't know if I believe everything O'Malley old us, but, well...what if she had something...Never mind."

"Let it go for now, Dev. If you really want to know, ask Cait. But let it go for now. There is some history, lots of it, but let it go until you talk to the women themselves."

"You know." It was not a question so Jamie did not respond. When Devin spoke again, it was with a little anger. "If this Dane hurts O'Malley, there won't be any hiding for her. I'll let it go for now, but I won't be put off long. Let me know what you find out."

After they hung up, Jamie decided to go to her office. He didn't figure it could hurt and it could get him in good with his mom if Dane would agree to help out with the kid. Smiling, he wondered if she would maybe have dinner with him too.

There was no one at the office when he got there. It was in a nice part of town and the building looked brand new. He walked around it for a few minutes then got back in his car. There had been a phone number on the door to call for emergencies. He pulled out his cell and called.

"Doctor Wallace answering service. How may I help you?"

Jamie thought he'd get a machine or maybe a recording, but not this cheery person on the other end. "My name is James Grant and I'd like to know when you expect Dr. Wallace back in the office?"

"I'm sorry, Mr. Grant, but I can't give you that information. I can tell you that Dr. Wallace will be in the office next week, and that she is booked up for a few weeks. I can make an appointment for you. Is this for your son or daughter?"

"Neither. I need to talk to her. She...she and I were in an accident the other night and she—"

"Oh, she told me about that. Yes, I remember where I've heard your name before. I'm so glad you're all right. Dane...err, Dr. Wallace will be out of town for a few more days. She had an emergency in California and she'll be back soon. Would you like to leave her a message? She calls in here several times a day to check."

California. Jamie suddenly knew that she was the specialist. He realized that the woman was still waiting for him to answer. "Yes, can you have her call me? I have a question I'd like her to answer for me." He gave her his cell phone number and his home number. Then gave his office number. "Tell her if I don't answer for her to leave a number and I'll call her back. Thanks."

Jamie didn't know why he was angry with Dane, but he was. He didn't like her giving false hope in child cases. He had seen enough in his lifetime with his mother working in the different state departments dealing with children and less desirable types to know what sort of people fed off them. Lawyers and scumbags who would make a quick buck off others' pain. He wondered if she charged for her "advice" and looked up at the building in front of him. Yeah, he thought, probably a bundle.

He was just sitting down to his dinner when his phone rang. Looking at the blocked caller ID, he nearly didn't answer it, but did anyway.

"Grant." Taking a huge bite of pizza, he waited for the person to speak and was wondering if it was one of those telemarketers that had the computer dial the number and then expected you to wait until they got to you.

"It's Dane Wallace, Mr. Grant. What can I do for you?" His mouth full and burning the crap out of him, he suddenly felt stupid. And for some reason, that made him angry and snappy.

"How's the weather in California, Dr. Wallace? Is it all right for searching for missing children in the woods? Or is that beneath you and your talents?"

Her hiss of breath had him feeling ashamed. He nearly told her he was sorry when she came back at him.

"Dead children who have been mutilated by their loved ones never has good weather, Mr. Grant, but I thank you for asking. Perhaps when they find the body of the six-year-old that her father says he raped then murdered, I'll make sure I note the sunny conditions and report it back to you as your earliest convenience. If all you called about was that, then I think we're through here. Good day."

The connection was cut off in a heartbeat and he put his phone on the table. It was that or throw it and he was sure that the shop would not be very happy if he did. He had been an ass. A prick and an ass. Christ, his mother was going to kill him and he deserved it. No longer hungry, he had them box up his dinner and left. When he got home, he turned on the news and waited for the reports to come on about the missing little girl and the daddy who had killed her.

Chapter 5

Dane put her phone in her pocket and stood next to the tent just outside the site where little Mercedes Evans was being dug up. Her father had confessed after he'd been arrested and had told them where she was. Dane had already told Markus, but they needed to have the father confess for the record. It was horrific work and though Dane knew the extent of her injuries intimately, she was still shocked at the little body when it was pulled from the shallow grave.

She didn't even wonder how the man she had just hung up on had figured out what people had been wondering about for years. She just knew that Detective Grant had told him her story and from there she didn't know, but he did not strike her as stupid. The tears threatened again, but she blinked them away.

It hurt to be thought of the way he did about her. But it hurt more coming from him for some reason. He had been so kind to her in the hospital and she had felt his sincerity too. When Markus went to the cameras to make a statement, Dane stepped back and faded into the background. She was on her way to the airport when he called her.

"I can't thank you enough, Dane. We couldn't have nailed him without the body and I doubt he'd have confessed without the extra that you gave us. Mercedes was just as you said she'd be, I'm sorry to say."

"Me too. I'm going home. And I'm not...please try to not call me for a few weeks, Markus. I really need to detox from this and to set up my practice. I have to have some sort of normal life. I can't keep...it takes too much from me. I can't keep doing this all the time."

"I know, baby. I'm sorry. Why don't you meet a nice man and settle down, have a few hundred babies and raise them to be nice people? There has to be someone out there to appreciate a beautiful woman like you. I know I would if you'd have me."

He had asked her out so many times over the years, but she had always said no. He was just not what she was looking for in a person to spend her life with. She was not sure if there was such a man, but she was not going to settle. Not this time. Once was enough.

"I'll talk to you sometime. And Markus? Thanks. You're a great friend." She closed her phone before he could answer her. More tired than she'd ever been, she was nearly fully asleep when the cab driver pulled up in front of the airport.

On Saturday morning, she was in the yard pulling weeds when Pi came out. She had a message from the police department and they would like for her to come by as soon as she could.

"Call them back and tell them I'm busy. Unless they want to arrest me, I don't have anything to say to them. I've filed my report on what happened at the Quad and they can fuck off."

"Missy Dane, you should have soap in your tongue. That man, Tucker, he say tell you that it important. You come down or he come here. I no think that good, so I tell him you come there."

"Pi, please tell me he didn't call and you told him this address? Please. I told you it's important that no one know where we live. I explained that as a doctor, it's important that I keep the house separate from the office, didn't I?"

"Yes, Missy Dane. He not have address. He hinted, but I no take the worm. I never said, promise. You go there now? You pick up fake Chinese on way back. I need to try other place before I open restaurant with real food. Shoo, shoo. Garden be here when you come back."

Dane was pulling into the lot when she realized that Pi had mentioned restaurant and wondered where that had come from. Laying her head on the steering wheel, Dane tried to imagine Pi trying to run a restaurant with American employees trying to understand what she said even half the time. Dane was still chuckling when she got out of the car.

~~~

That was how Jamie saw her when she walked toward the station. She was standing in the afternoon sun with a pretty sundress on her shoulders, kissed by the sun, smiling.

"She's here. She just got out of her car. If this doesn't work, Devin, I'm going to kill you. Mom said she'd talk to her first. This is really stupid." Jamie never took his eyes off the woman nearly to the door below them.

"It has to work. Mom needs her, the evidence is here. If it's not her, then we made a mistake, but you know as well as I do that Mom believes it's her. She's the specialist from out west and she needs her."

Cait and their mom walked in a few seconds later. His mom was still angry with him for what he'd done and said to Dane, but she loved him and would eventually forgive him — he hoped. Cait was pacing the room and he wondered what Dane would say to her too. This whole thing was a really stupid idea and he suddenly knew it was going to go badly for them all.

"I think we should call this off. This is really—" Dane walked in, cutting him off. He could tell immediately that she was not happy to see them. When she stopped in the doorway, Captain Tucker, Donny to his friends, gave her a little nudge to get her moving again.

"If this is some sort of joke, then I'm not laughing. You said this was about the case with Mr. Grant. You never said neither his family nor him was going to be here. I'd like to go, please. I have things I want to do; a root canal or a pap smear would be better than this."

"Please sit down, Dr. Wallace. Or is it Dr. Messenger? Either way, we need your help. I realize that some of my family has been…let's say, less than civil to you, but there is a problem and I know you can help me." Jamie blushed at his mom's pointed look.

"What on earth do you think I can…ah, I see." She stared at him and Jamie began to squirm in his seat. "You don't believe me, so why are you even here? Never mind. It doesn't matter. What do you have, Mrs. Parker."

"You know me? Well, I mean, I…okay. I have a missing child, well, three as a matter of fact. Their father says the mother took them, the mother says he did. Regardless of who did what, they're still missing and have been for several weeks."

"You know that the longer they're gone, the more likely they are dead, don't you? I can't help you without something that belongs to each child." She looked at Devin, anger evident in her voice. "What are you doing here, Mr. Grant? Do you believe I'd do something to your family that you'd need to sue me for?"

"I'm here to negotiate your fee, doctor. And to give you this. It's an agreement that states whatever you say in here, whatever information you give us, is confidential and will not go beyond these doors. Everyone in here has signed it."

"Even you, detective? That must have hurt. Knowing that you have to keep quiet this time. I'll talk to you, Mrs. Parker, and to you, Mr. Grant, but the other two leave or I do. Mr. Grant" — she pointed at Jamie — "here has made his position on what I do very clear to me and I don't need the negative energy when I help — if I help."

"Dane, I'm sorry. I had no right to —" Jamie started only to be cut off.

"You're absolutely right, Mr. Grant. You had no right to judge me or what I can or can't do. If you want me to help, then I'd like you to leave. Now, please."

Jamie looked at her and saw the tears in her eyes. He'd hurt her. Hurt her badly, and he couldn't even begin to tell her how sorry he was. He stood and walked to the door with Cait.

Cait turned back to Dane. "I'm sorry too. You have no idea just how much I've regretted the way things ended between us. How I felt when I found you there. Hunter is dead, I know you remember him. I killed him several months ago when he killed my Uncle Paddy and Aunt Dee. I know it's no excuse, but I was so young and so were you. Hunter seemed to know just...I'm so sorry."

Jamie followed her out and held her while she cried. When she went to the bathroom, he called Spencer and asked him to come and get her, that she was upset.

"It's that damned woman again, isn't it? I told O'Malley to stay here that there was no reason to be near her. She thinks to talk her into forgiving her. As far as I'm concerned, the bitch can just bite me. It's been ten years, give it up already."

Jamie let go on his brother what he wanted to say to himself. "You think this has been easy for her, for Dane? You think it's been easy knowing that the one group of people you were taught to trust betrayed you, let another child die because they were too pigheaded to listen to you? How do you think she's lived with herself knowing that she held that little girl's life in her hands and couldn't make anyone believe her, help her? Yeah, it's been ten years, but do you think you'd forget if Cait hadn't been able to save Meggie? That you knew that someone out there had the ability to save her and they didn't because others were too stupid to listen to her?"

Jamie closed his phone and bounced it in his hand several times before he did what he'd wanted to for several days. He threw it across the room with enough force to shatter it and dent the wallboard beneath it. Pieces of it sprayed around the room a good ten feet from impact. Someone clapping their hands brought him around quickly.

"Do you feel better? I know I would if I could do that. But I have enough trouble with keeping phones around without destroying them myself. Spencer already complains about my inability to have one for more than two weeks." Cait moved in the room and sat on the chair closest to her. "I take it you were speaking to my husband. I hope you gave him an earful. He's been telling me for days that I need to move on from this girl. I can't, Jamie. I let her down, or that little girl. I'll never forgive myself for that until Dane does."

"I know, sweetie. Me too. I didn't believe you at first. Now...now I'm not sure. I called her the other day. She was in California with another case. I was...I wasn't very nice. I

50

don't know what it is about her that made me want to lash out, but I did. I wish I knew what to do too."

Spencer came and got Cait, but neither man spoke. Jamie was sorry for that, but then he knew that once they got home, Cait would tell him. Or she'd hurt him. Either way, Jamie would get a call. He sat in one of the chairs and waited until they were done in the office. He was going to have a few words with Dr. Wallace before she left if he had to throw her to the floor and hold her there.

His mother had called her family by the Messenger name. He remembered her name had been that as a kid and wondered at the change. He knew from Devin that Dane had been in China since a week after she'd been found in the garage. She had come back to the States a few times over the years, once when her mother died then again when her grandmother had passed away. Jamie also knew that she had inherited from her grandmother and not her mother. The Messenger estate had been worth millions and the older lady, Mrs. Sharp, had inherited from her daughter. Jamie figured that the grandmother had left her monies to Dane. He was not sure what the going rate for finding people was, but he was sure it paid quite well.

When the door opened an hour later, Jamie stood up. He'd been about to go to the bathroom and was now glad that he had not. If he hadn't been there, he was sure Dane would have left. He wasn't even sure she was going to stay long enough to talk to him now.

"Thank you, my dear. You don't...I thank you so much for what you've done for me. If you ever need anything, just let me know. You'll have it," his mom was saying when Jamie walked up behind Dane.

"Just remember our promise, Mrs. Parker. I'm sorry about everything. I wish I could have had better news."

Suddenly, Dane swayed and Jamie scooped her up before she hit the floor. "I'm fine, please put me down. Of all the nerve, do you usually pick women up like a sack of potatoes?"

"Yes, especially when they practically fall into my arms. Now hush and let me hold you until you get some color back in your face. You look like death warmed over."

"Such a charmer. I bet women just fall over themselves to get a piece of you, don't they? You baboon, put me down before you break your back."

"I said hush. Christ, woman, what the hell is wrong with you? Mom, can you please go and get her something to drink? Devin, don't just stand there, open the door. I'll take her in here until she looks better."

He rushed her back into the room they'd been in and sat in one of the chairs with Dane now sitting on his lap. When she started to struggle to get down, he pressed her against his erection and whispered in her ear so that only she could hear him.

"You're making me as hard as rock moving your ass all over me. If you don't sit still, I'm going to throw you over my lap and spank you. Not that I think that'll make me any less hard, but it will be a sight more enjoyable than you just wiggling on me." She stilled instantly. "Good girl."

When she looked at him, her eyes were wide and dark. He was not sure if it was from desire of anger, but he was willing to bet it was the latter of the two. It didn't really matter, she was lovely anyway. Before his mother came back, Jamie quickly brushed his mouth over hers and took advantage of her stunned silence. When his mother returned with a cola, Dane's cheeks were redder, but Jamie knew it was probably due more to the kiss and comment than anything else.

"I'll take you home. You shouldn't drive like this. I have my car right here. Maybe we can get some dinner too." Manipulative? Yes, but he wanted to talk to her.

"Oh Jamie, what a nice thought. Of course you'll take her home. And dinner, we could all use some, I'm sure. My treat. I think Chinese is what we need. I love it."

"No. Thanks, but no. I can get myself home. I'll be fine now as soon as this idiot lets go of me. Do you mind?" She started to wiggle again and stopped when he pressed her bottom hard over his cock. He might have laughed if it did not hurt so badly.

"Nope. And I'm taking you home. We'll get something to eat, then I'll take you home and you can feed me some dessert there. It's the least you can do for making things so…hard for me." Devin burst out laughing when Dane turned bright red. Margaret looked at both of them, confused, but let it go.

"Come along then. Devin, I'll ride with you. Jamie, you and Dane ride in your car and follow us, all right?"

"Mom, give us a minute, will you? I have to tell Dane a couple of things. We won't be long." When the door shut behind his mother and brother, she became a wild cat and threw them both to the floor in her effort to get off his lap.

It took everything he had not to hurt her and more not to let her hurt him. Finally, he had to lie over her, his body firmly between her legs so she could not kick him again, to make her stop. Pulling her hands up over her head, he waited until she wore herself out.

"Are you finished yet? You are a hell cat, aren't you? Why don't you want me to take you home?"

"Get off me, you lug! I don't want anyone to know where I live. Is that plain…you're touching me." It took his mind a few seconds to catch up with her words.

"So I am. I'd like to touch you more, Dane. I'd very much like to taste your mouth." He eased his head toward hers and gently brushed his mouth over hers. He didn't pull all the way back, but he did enough to look at her. "Was that all right, Dane? Did it hurt?"

"No. Please don't do it again. You can't want to kiss me. I'm not...I'm a freak and people don't kiss freaks, James."

"Hummm, I like you calling me James. And I do want to kiss you again, Dane. I want to kiss you very badly. Will you give me your mouth, love? Let me taste you?"

He didn't let her answer but brushed his mouth over hers again, then again. The third time he did, he pulled her lower lip into his mouth and nipped at it. When she sighed softly, he kissed her gently.

Her mouth was soft and when he pulled back to look down at her again, he groaned when her tongue came out and licked at her lips. This time, he was not as gentle. This time, he tasted paradise.

When she opened her mouth under his, he cupped her neck and tilted her slightly to deepen the kiss. His tongue swept across hers and in seconds, she was sliding her tongue with his in a sensual dance that had him wanting more. When her legs came up and wrapped around his hips, he reached down, pulled her harder against him, and rocked into her. Sliding his mouth along her jaw to her neck, he nipped at the frantically beating pulse there and suckled it into his mouth before moving back to her mouth. His hand was just slipping under her blouse when someone pounded on the door behind them.

Chapter 6

Dane looked up at the man over her. Her heart was pounding in her chest and she could barely take a deep breath without smelling him, smelling them. He was looking at her as if he wanted to murder someone.

"Jamie! Spencer called. Cait's in labor. We have to go. Now!" Devin said on the other side of the door. She could hear the panic in his voice and the urgency.

"She'll be all right. Both of them will. Spencer is holding his child, his son. They both will hold him and take him home. They'll be fine." He looked at her oddly then pulled away. Still sitting on his heels, he looked down at her. She turned away and began pulling her into herself.

"Don't, Dane. Don't do this. Something happened here. I don't…why could I touch you? What made me so different?"

"I don't…you should go. I'm going to go home. I hope everything is all right with your family." When she started to pull away from him and crawl away, he pinned her back to the floor.

"Look at me. Dane, look at me. We aren't finished here. Something is…I didn't hurt you. I want to know why."

"Damn it, Jamie, come on. Mom is in the car. Now, let's go." Devin had opened the door then and turned his back on them. "I'm sorry, but Spencer said that she was bleeding. And he was worried. I'm sorry, Dane."

When Jamie pulled away this time, she got up too. Her legs were slightly wobbly, but that could be from anything. She moved to the table to get her bag when Jamie came up behind her.

"Dane, give me a way to contact you, please. I want to see you again. I want to talk to you, about us, about this."

"I'll contact you. There is no us, Mr. Grant. I'm not going to have an affair with you or anyone. You should go. Your family is waiting."

"Damn it, Dane, this is—"

"Jamie, now. You can fix this later. We have to go." Jamie pulled her around and kissed her again. It was not like before, soft and searching. This was hard and demanding, bruising almost. Then he was gone.

Dane sat in the chair, collapsed really, and laid her head on the table. Before she realized it, she was crying softly. She heard someone knock on the door and she sat up, but didn't turn to the opening.

"Dr. Wallace? The man downstairs asked for someone to take you home. I've got a car out front for you. We don't normally do this, but Jamie and me, we go way back and he—"

"No problem, officer. I have my own car. I'll be fine. Thank you for your help. I'll be going now. I'm sorry to have made you wait."

Quickly gathering her things, she rushed out the door and into the lot. It took her several tries before she got the key in the lock and a few to get it in the ignition. She was on her way home when she realized that she didn't watch to see if she was being followed. It took her three turns to figure out that she was and then three frantic moves off and on the highway to lose them. She would have to be more careful in the future. It did not pay to have people know where you lived.

Pi was in the kitchen when she pulled into the garage and walked into the house. She looked pissed. Dane was tired and sore, but she sat down and let Pi feed her. If asked, she was sure she would not have been able to tell anyone what she ate, nor a single word her and Pi had talked about. As soon as she could escape, she went to her office in the basement.

The townhouse they were renting was not all that great, but it was home for now. As soon as possible, they had planned to buy a home, one that they picked out together. Pi wanted a huge kitchen and a place to plant a garden. Dane wanted a pool and a separate place she could go that no one had ever touched. She pulled these plans out now.

The building that she wanted would not be huge, big enough to have a single room and a bath. No kitchen or closest and no phone. She wanted one wall to be floor to ceiling windows that would open in the warmer months and faced a wooded area. Dane even knew what kind of wooded area she wanted. Pines and evergreen along with maples and oaks and trees that would bloom in the spring and color in the fall, something she could look at all the time and not feel the drab of winter or the heat of summer — a forest for year round. Walls of white, carpet too. Somewhere she would be able to go and have nothing. No sound, no noise, no voices, and especially no emotions. Her own paradisiacal getaway.

Sighing, she reached for her bag and pulled out the bag that Mrs. Parker had given her at the station. She didn't get anything from any of the items that she brought in, but Mrs. Parker knew that she might not. She had told Dane that the things felt too new, too stiff to be that of three little children.

The first one was a shirt. Laying it onto the desk, Dane pressed her hands over the material and closed her eyes.

She had to sort through all the people who had touched it. Mrs. Parker, a woman, and three men. There were several children as well. None related and Dane assumed that it was from the people shopping, people touching the shirt to check sizes, fit, or just to move it. She was ready to fold it back into the bag when she touched the sleeve. A jolt of pain hit her. Carefully, she picked up the phone without breaking contact with the sleeve and called Pi.

"Pi, I'm going under. It's seven o'clock, correct?"

"Missy Dane, it's late. Please tomorrow. You be hurt enough. Wait for tomorrow."

"I can't, Pi. I wish I could, but it's too late. Will you watch for me, please?"

"You know I will. You be my sandwich winner. I need you to bring home bacon. Don't understand that, why people eat bacon beyond me, but you be mine. I watch. I have contact if you don't come back to me. You come back, okay?"

"Yes, I'll come back. Four hours, no more. Then you come and get me." Hanging up the phone, Dane closed her eyes and fell into the feeling.

It was not the child that she felt, but a woman. Pain and hate, then sorrow. Profound sorrow emanated from the spot. Images flashed by, a boy then a man. A girl then the man again. Blood. Breathless running. Pain again, her own this time and not general. Hunger. Darkness. The woman, this time an image, dark hair—no, wet hair, blood, eyes blue, bruises, then she was gone. A boy, small and huddled in a corner, blood pouring from his head, and his arm lay at an odd angle. Moving closer, Dane could see that he was no longer breathing. His neck had been broken. Sorrow again then deep, deep depression. Then black.

~~~

Jamie was sitting next to his brothers when Damon came out. Something had happened. He knew it as sure as he was sitting there. His mom knew too. She started crying softly as Byron held her.

"The cord is wrapped around his throat. Every contraction strangles him more and more. They're going to have to perform an emergency c-section to save him. Cait is losing blood and they are worried about her too. It...it doesn't look good for either of them. Spencer is frantic. He's...Mom, he needs you."

"She said they would be fine. Dane. She said they'd be all right that they would both take him home," Jamie said.

"That's right. In the hospital when Spencer touched her, she told me to tell him that everyone would be all right that he would hold his son. Mom?" Damon asked his mother.

"Go! Tell her. Cait will believe you, tell them. Hurry and bring my grandson into this world." Damon took off down the hall and disappeared behind a door.

The waiting was long and tense. Twice, a nurse came out to give them updates. Once to say that the doctor was here and he was prepping for surgery. The next time she came out to say that the operation had begun. She could not tell them anything more. She told them that she had not been in the room. She was at the desk and relaying the information they gave her. For another hour and a half they waited until Spencer came out with Damon.

"She's going to be okay. So is my son, our son. He's bruised and he'll be sore for a little while, but he's fine. They're both going to be fine. I have a son." Spencer picked up his daughter, Meggie, and cried in her arms as she held him.

In seconds, they were wrapped around him, all of them holding him, patting his back. Meggie patted each one on the head and kissed their cheeks. That was how the doctor found them the entire Grant clan, standing in the middle of the waiting room in a large, loving group. Jamie was sure the man thought they were nuts.

"We'll leave her in recovery for a few more hours then move her to her room. Baby boy Grant is going to be in the Neonatal area for a few days just to be sure. They both are doing great. Mrs. Grant has lost some blood, but with rest and plenty of fluids, she'll be her old cranky self in about a week. I don't know what you said to her, but that was the turning point. She had all but given up in there and we both know it. Thanks, Damon, you saved my patient. If you need me, I'll be in my office until morning."

They took turns going in to see the little boy. No one could hold him just yet. The doctor was afraid to over stimulate him and he needed to rest. The bruise was dark against his fair skin, but he was breathing on his own. Meggie touched her brother and he stretched out to her and made her smile. Margaret took a few pictures without her flash to show Dan and the boys later. Then, when Cait was taken to her room, they converged in mass to see her.

"He's lovely, honey. Looks just like Spencer did when he was born, only I think this one is a bit more handsome. And the bruise will fade and you won't be able to tell a thing."

"What's his name? You've been keeping this huge secret for months now. What are we going to call him?" Byron asked as he held Taylor.

"He's Spencer Patrick O'Malley James Grant. We're going to call him Paddy for short."

"Holy crap, Spence, that poor kid. He'll have to be tough in order to carry a name like that around. And Paddy?

Sheesh, you might as well hang a 'kick me' sign on him right now." Byron laughed. Cait smacked him on the shoulder and kissed him. Jamie was about to say something just as mean when his phone rang.

"Mister Dane friend? You come here now. I can't get door open. You come now."

"I'm sorry, who is this? What's happened to Dane?" Jamie looked at the caller ID and since it was blocked, he still did not know who she was.

"Pi Chang. Missy Dane my bacon. You come now. She sleep hard. I can't wake her. Come now."

Jamie looked at his brothers. "I'm coming. Call an ambulance. I'll be right there. Give me her address and I'm on my way."

Jamie was moving to the elevator as Pi gave him the address and when the doors opened, three of his brothers were with him, Damon, Byron, and Devin. His mother was running down the hall as well.

"I don't know what's happened. I don't think you need to go with me. Pi said she —"

"Shut up and push the damned button. We're going. Byron, you drive. Damon, you make sure you have your bag of tricks. Devin, you take care of the police when we get there. That poor girl. She said it was going to be difficult reading those things. I just hope she's all right." His mother could work for any corporate office and have it whipped into shape by end of work day. Jamie smiled.

It took them four minutes to get there. Dane lived just across the street from the hospital. The ambulance showed up just as they were getting out of the car. Jamie ran into the townhouse and down the stairs to where he could hear someone screaming. Pi, or who he assumed was her, was pounding on the door and crying.

"I can't make her wake. She said four hours, no more. I only wait ten minute too many. I not kill her, did I? She my bacon. I need my bacon."

Jamie moved the hysterical woman out of the way and before he could slam himself, Byron stopped him.

"You'll break your shoulder. The three of us do this together on three. Three...two...one." The door did not stand a chance under their combined weight. It splintered and broke through and the three men when tumbling in. Jamie scrambled over to see to Dane.

She was lying in her chair, which was close to the desk. Her face was pale and her lips where blue. She was breathing, but it was faint and shallow. Tears had dried on her cheeks and there was a little blood on her lip. Damon had to ask him twice to move. His mother was talking to Pi and calming her down.

"This woman says she needs a cold shower. Mrs. Chang said to put Dane into a cold shower. There's a bathroom just over there."

"She scream, but you hold her till she wake. She mean when she wake, you no let her hurt you. She my bacon and I need her to be good."

Jamie turned to his brother. "Damon? Should we?"

"I don't know, Jamie. I don't know what's happened. But if this woman says it'll work, then she knows more than we know at this point. I'll take her in."

"No. I have her. Turn on the water. I'm going to strip down to my boxers. Be ready in case this doesn't work, okay?"

Jamie ended up in his jeans, taking everything out of them and picking Dane up. Her body was limp as she carried her into the bathroom and when he stepped into the stall, he nearly screamed himself from the cold temperature of the spray. As soon as the water hit Dane, she came screaming awake and fighting.

Chapter 7

Every time Dane looked at him, she was glaring a little harder. At least the shivers had stopped, Jamie noticed. And her lips were pinking up. He was sure the color in her cheeks was due more to the anger she was directing at him than the embarrassment or cold. He winked at her every time he caught her looking his way.

Pi and his mother were upstairs in the kitchen. Damon was talking with the medics and Devin was dealing with the police. Byron was talking quietly with Dane. Jamie had been ordered by Dane to stay away from her. He was going to give her five more minutes then he was going to haul her body up against his and kiss the daylights out of her then spank her ass. He glanced back at the broken door and shuddered again.

"Mr. Grant? The landlord says he's not paying for the damages and he wants to press charges against you and your brothers for breaking it down. I need to know what you want to do about it." This cop had just walked into the basement.

"See that man over there? He's my attorney. Talk to him." Jamie started over to Dane and stopped when she stood up.

"You stay away from me, Mr. Grant. The nerve bringing all these people in my home when it was—"

He had meant to talk to her. Had even meant to see if she was all right, or hurt in anyway first. But kissing her seemed much better the moment she opened her mouth. And holding her close was all he could think about. And when Dane wrapped her arms around his neck and pressed closer to him, he knew that he'd made the right decision. Hearing his brother chuckle did not even stop him from cupping her ass and bringing her tighter against him.

He tasted her mouth like a starved man. Her flavor and scent pulled at his senses, making him lightheaded and needy. When Dane's tongue slid into his mouth and tangled with his, he groaned and shifted her so that now she was between his legs, her soft folds hard against his erection. Everything in the room faded away as they explored each other. Byron tugging at his arm brought him back, reluctantly.

"Jamie, Mom's coming down. I'm reasonably sure you don't want to be lip-locked like you are when she gets here. She'll rip your ear off like she did that time she caught you necking in the back seat with Helen Smart."

Jamie pulled away, but did not let Dane go. He was still holding her when his mom entered the office basement with Pi right on her heels. He looked over at the two women and winked.

"Let me go, you ass. You jerk me around like I'm some sort of lost puppy. I have to go to the bathroom. By myself, thank you." He watched her walk away then sat next to his brother. Devin joined them a minute later.

"They're going to make her move out. He said he doesn't need this sort of thing going on around here. Dumbass. I told him that she was in trouble and he said to have her take her trouble elsewhere," Devin said, disgusted.

"I'll talk to her. She seems like a reasonable girl. Maybe we can find her a place to stay for a few days until things settle, maybe with Taylor and me. I don't like her staying here if this could happen again." Jamie just looked at Byron. For a reason he could not explain, he wanted to hit him.

"I'll take care of her. And if you don't mind, I want you to stay away from her. She's...she's..." She's what? Jamie thought.

"Ah. Well, why didn't you say so? By all means. I like her too. Does Mom know yet?" Jamie decided to ignore him and watched as Dane came toward them.

"Mr. Grant?"

All three of them turned to her and said, "What?"

Her low growl made all three of them laugh, but then they quickly turned it into a cough. He wondered why they did that. His brothers did it a lot, and him only recently. He wondered if it had anything to do with the women in their lives.

"The attorney. Sheesh, how many more of you are there? Devin Grant, please. May I have a word with you in private?"

The two of them walked to the other side of the room and then Devin motioned to his mother to join them a minute later. When Margaret started crying, Jamie walked over with Byron. Something was wrong.

"I'm sorry, Mrs. Parker. I can tell you where...go away. I didn't want to talk to you. This is between your mom and me." Dane looked at him, scared now. No, more like she was terrified. He knew it had something to do with what had happened today.

"No. What's going on? I want to know why you were so comatose that you couldn't hear someone pounding on the door. Why you had to be shocked to come around. I want to know what happened to make you so afraid to say anything to me."

"You don't get to...I found him all right? One of the little boys your mom asked me about. His mother killed him then buried him under a big tree not far from the trailer where he lived. I saw it, her throwing him against the counter, her picking up the shovel and hitting him over and over until his head was mashed in. Then she wrapped him in a black trash bag and took him outside and buried him with the same shovel she killed him with. I felt it, the pain, the sorrow. I felt each strike of the heavy shovel. I felt each time the shovel vibrated against his tiny...I'm going to be sick." She darted away and when Jamie went to follow, Devin held him back.

"Not yet. She needs to deal with this. And I need to tell you something. Dane told us today some of what she does when she does this. How much it takes out of her. You don't believe her, she told me. I don't know if I do either. But if that little boy is where she said, she's made a believer out of me. She needs support, not someone who is only in this for sex. You understand what I'm saying to you?"

"You're telling me that if I can't be there for her now, to back the fuck out. Yeah, I get it. But I didn't ask for, nor do I need your advice. I'm going to see if she's all right."

Jamie went to the bathroom door and waited for her. He saw his brother talking to the police. Jamie knew that one of them was a good friend of Devin's. The police and the medics left a few minutes later. Pi took his mother upstairs again and Byron was on the phone. When the door lock clicked, he stood up and watched her come out of the room.

"I'm drained, Mr. Grant. I don't think I can deal with anything else today. I'll be fine. Why don't you all go home? Pi will be with me."

"I can't. I need to hold you. Dane, talk to me, please? I want to help. I want to understand what happened here today. Why were you so out of it?"

He didn't think she was going to answer, but when she did, he was surprised. "If you don't mind staying after...later, I'll tell you. Right now, I can't. Not right now. Okay?"

"Yes. For now anyway. Dane, will you let me hold you, please?"

"Let me change first. I'm cold and wet. I think Pi is fixing something to eat. Go up to the kitchen and I'll be down shortly." He pulled her to him for a quick kiss and then let her go. He didn't know which of them was more surprised, her because he let her go, or him because he could. He made his way to the kitchen with his family.

"It not big kitchen, but it work. You like food, I cook. Sit! I make dinner. I make real Chinese food, you eat," Pi was saying as he walked in and sat at the table.

When Margaret asked if she could help, all three boys yelled "no" all at once. "I'm not that bad of a cook. I just choose not to. I know how to peel an onion, you know."

"I have herbs you crush. You no get in my way. Missy Dane friend, you go and take care of Missy Dane. She need you. I see you look at her."

Jamie blushed bright red and left the kitchen to find Dane when his brothers started in on him. He found her coming down the stairs and met her there. She looked lost.

"What does your family think of me now? I'm betting they think I'm some sort of fool and an idiot. I don't blame them. But I can't help what happens when I...is Pi cooking? She does that when she's nervous." He noticed she would not look at him.

"I don't think they think anything of you. And yes, Pi is cooking for us. I think you're right. She needs this after what happened. Are you all right, Dane?" She nodded, but still wouldn't look at him. "Dane?"

"Mr. Grant, I don't know how Pi got in touch with you, but I assure you that I will make it so she never bothers you again like this. She shouldn't have called anyone. Especially…especially not you. She won't do it again."

"You called me James when I kissed you, when I nearly made love to you. I'd like for you to call me that again. And for you to look at me, please. I'm glad she called me." He took a step up the stairs toward her and watched as she took one back. "I don't want to think what might have happened if she hadn't."

"That was a mistake too. I should never have…we shouldn't have kissed or the rest. Your family doesn't believe in me. You don't even believe in me. I think it's better if we keep this on a professional level." Two more steps up to her three back. "Will you stop that?"

"No. I don't think so. I want to take you to your bedroom and make love to you. Several times, as a matter of fact. I want to be buried deep inside of you when I come, feeling you come around me and over me. Whether or not my family believes in you or not is a moot point." He took another step. "Do you want me to, Dane?"

"You don't know what happens when I…I can't help that I can do this. I…Mr. Grant, I'm…"

"Dane, you call me Mr. Grant again and I'll paddle your butt. I'm Jamie, or James. I want to hear you say it."

They were at the top of the stairs now and he could see three closed doors behind her. One had to lead to the bathroom he'd heard running when he was in the kitchen, the other two, bedrooms. He wanted to find hers soon and stretch her out on it with him over her.

70

"You…you need to leave. I have to work tomorrow and I—" He touched her shoulders with just the tips of his fingers. He watched as her eyes darkened and her pulse picked up.

"Which room is yours?" Jamie ran his hands down her arms and to her hands where he laced her fingers with his. He pulled both their hands behind her, pressed her hard against him, and licked along the seam of her lips.

"This isn't…please, you don't want to do this. I'm not going to…oh, James, please." When she tilted her head and exposed her neck for him, he ran his tongue along the long column and nipped at her beating pulse.

Releasing her hands, he cupped her ass again and picked her up. Her legs wrapped around his hips as her arms encircled his neck. Jamie covered her mouth with his and ate at her as he moved forward toward the wall across from the stairs. Riding her up and down his cock, he pressed harder into her when her back touched the wall. Using it as leverage, he pulled her shirt from her jeans and ran his hands under to touch her bare skin.

Heat and soft skin, his hands could not stop touching her. Lifting his hands higher, Jamie cupped her breasts and moaned at the weight of them in his palms. Using his thumbs, he slid under her bra and rubbed her hard nipples. Need to taste them had him tear from her mouth and pull one into his mouth through the shirt and bra and bite. Her hiss of approval gave him all the encouragement he needed and he started working at the buttons while he nuzzled at her full breast and pulled at the other nipple with his thumb and finger.

"I need to taste you. I want to suckle at your breast and taste you. Help me, baby."

She smacked his hands away and lifted her blouse up, unclasping the closure in the front of her lacy blue bra. As soon as it was open, he pushed the edges open and rubbed his nose over the hard peak then took it deep into his mouth. She was rocking hard against him and with every push from the wall into his body, he countered with a rock back. When he bit down on her nipple, she moaned and growled at him.

"Please, James. If you don't stop, I'm going to come right now. And your family is right downstairs. You have to stop now before it's too late."

"It's already too late. Come for me, baby. Come right now. I'll catch you. I want to feel you come."

He rocked harder and with his free hand, he reached between them and pressed his thumb against her clit hard and then harder still. When her body stiffened and he felt her start to shatter around him, he covered her mouth with his and captured her screams.

Jamie kept rocking into her heat. His cock ached to be released and driven into her hard and fast. He held her as she came down, held her as her body became relaxed, sated and limp against him. When she rested her head on his shoulder, he let her legs fall to the floor, but he did not let go of her. Soon her breathing became normal and with it, came her withdrawal from him. He leaned back and pulled her body to his again.

"No. Look at me. Dane, look at me. Don't pull away. Talk to me, baby. Tell me what's wrong."

She looked up at him then, her eyes full of sorrow and hurt. He wondered what he'd done then realized that this was old pain. She had been hurt by someone; someone had hurt her during sex or about sex. She was ashamed too, he could see that now. He wanted to find whoever it was and pound the shit out of them.

"I need to tell you something. Show you something about me. I've…you need to see this before we can…before we have any…before, you know."

"Make love? You meant before we make love? All right. I'll stay after my family leaves. Will you talk to me then? I want us to be together, baby."

"Yes. Then if you still want to…if you don't freak out, then we can have sex. But I'll understand if you need to leave. Its…it's happened before."

He was going to find this man who had hurt her and beat the shit out of him. Whoever he was, where ever he was, Jamie was going to beat the guy until he could not walk then start all over. They held hands as they entered the kitchen.

Chapter 8

To say that Dane was embarrassed would have been a gross understatement. And she did not know how they knew, but his brothers kept looking at her as though she had a sign that said "just had incredible climax" on her. Pi was making rice and cutting up vegetables and talking a mile a minute. Dane had been living with her for so long she no longer had to translate in her head what Pi was saying, but the Grants seemed lost.

"She wants to know if you want any egg in your rice. I know asking if you have yellow slime in your diet is a little weird, but she means well. We usually speak in Chinese when we're alone."

"Oh, well. Pi, you fix it however you wish. I love Chinese food. Morgan will be so jealous. But now that we're on the subject of translator, could you explain what she means when she calls you her bacon? I've been trying to sort it out and I just…she does have a way with words doesn't she?"

"I say Missy Dane my bacon. She bring it home and I cook it. I no have job, I her…what are I Missy Dane? And be nice. We have people."

"You're my companion. And my friend. I simply couldn't make it without you. Although there are days that I think I'd like to try. Pi, how did you get Mr. Grant's phone number to call him?"

"Service lady. She call me with numbers to have when you get them. I have list of them. I keep for you and me. I have many Grants and he have nice name. So when you not open door, I call. He come fast. You keep him."

Dane flushed again. She should have asked later. When Jamie came up behind her and wrapped his arm around her waist and pulled her close, she felt heat rush her veins and her pussy flood with need. When she started to pull away from him, to try and get some distance, he pulled her back.

"I want you to keep me too. If I promise not to come too fast, will you?" he whispered in her ear. Then he bit her lobe gently. It was everything she could do not to turn around and bite him back.

"Dane, the police are going to talk to the family again. I want to thank you for looking into this, but next time, please make sure you aren't locked in when you do it. I have never been so afraid in my life," Devin was telling her.

Jamie pulled her into his lap and before she could get away, he pressed his erection into her. Her body flushed again. Bryon grinned at her. She didn't have any brothers, but she was pretty sure that if this one had been hers, he would have had a permanent black eye.

"I wasn't. Locked in, I mean. That door sticks all the time. The landlord won't fix it. He said that the basement isn't made for an office, that I'm lucky that he lets me run an office from there anyway. We were looking for a house to buy—Pi was looking. I have things I...I'm just her bacon. But things have changed now."

"About that. It seems you're being evicted. Mr. Camel said that you have thirty days to leave the premises or he'll have you removed. It's within his rights, I'm afraid. He said that you don't have a lease and that you don't have a security deposit." Dane looked at Pi who paled slightly. "I'll do everything I can to help you. There are several houses in foreclosure right now, so you could get a good deal. Just let me know what you are looking for and I'll do some searches."

"Mr. Grant, I appreciate your help, but Pi and I have been talking. I don't think this is...I thought things would be different this time. I, we've decided that we're going back to China. I thank you for—"

"I don't think so. No, I just don't think so. I've just...Mom, I'm going to let Pi and Dane move in with me. I was going to talk to you about it later, but things have...you aren't going back. I can't let you."

"Wow, there buck-o. I make my own decisions. You have no say in where I live and what I do. If I wanted someone to dictate my life and how I run it, I would have stayed married. Now, thank you all for coming to help us, but I think you should leave. Pi, I'll be in my office." Dane stood and was nearly to the basement stairs when she was scooped up and thrown over a shoulder. "Put me down, you idiot. I am not— that fucking hurt." She rubbed her abused ass and watched as his family came out of the kitchen and looked on as he started up the stairs to the upper floors.

"Is anyone going to stop this? He is acting like a...like a—"

"A man who knows what he wants? Yes, I see that. James Grant, don't you beat her too badly. I'd like to have a word with her in a few days. Come on, sons, we should help Pi clean up the kitchen and—"

"Mrs. Parker, I helped you! Make him behave, please. This is none of his business."

"Oh dear, yes, you're right. Jamie, use a condom. There, sweetheart, I've helped, and I'll tell you now, I think he's made it his business."

~~~

Jamie could not believe his mother and decided that he was going to send her flowers tomorrow for her "help." Smiling, Jamie opened the first door. He did not know why, but he was sure he had found Dane's. Moving inside, he closed and locked the door behind him.

The room was white. There were no other colors in the room with the exception of the furniture. Everything else, the walls, the carpet, and the comforter were all white. He stood in the middle of the room and looked around. There was nothing on the dressers; no pictures, not even a brush. The bed had a white canopy and white duster; there was even a white rug next to it. The lamp next to the bed was devoid of color as well. He knew that this was not just a place for her to sleep. It was also her place to come and unwind.

"I'm going to put you down and you'll listen to me before you get all pissy, all right?" She did not answer so he swatted her again. He would have to talk to Byron later about this. He did not want to dominate Dane, but the thought of spanking her pink had his cock twitch in his jeans.

"When I get down, you had better run. I'm going to hurt you in ways you've never dreamed of. I want you to put me down right fucking now!"

Her voice was low, but he could hear her intent. He thought she might just do it. Smiling, he reached up and rubbed her ass then moved his hand between her legs. When she parted her legs for him, he knew he had her.

"I'm going to make love to you, Dane. I'm going to lap up your pussy until you scream my name, then I'm going to lose myself inside of you. I've never wanted a woman like I do you. I find it hard to think when you're around."

She was quiet for so long he thought she would not answer. "I have to show you something. I...you may not want to...put me down, James. I'll show you why we can't be close."

She stood before him when he slid her down his body and looked up at him. He wanted to take her into his arms and kiss her, but he knew also that this was important and he wanted to do this right. She looked so sad, though, that he was hard pressed not to just leave her alone as she had asked.

"Lie on the bed, but take off your shirt first. I have to be able to touch you to show you. Is that all right?"

He unbuttoned his shirt and threw it in the small chair next to a vanity. There was nothing on it but a white book. The chair a white cover and pillow. He moved to the bed and helped her pull the blanket down to the foot and was not surprised by the sheets. He lay down without saying a word.

"I'm going to touch you. But you can't touch me until I tell you. This isn't a power trip, but a way to not overload you. As soon as you've had too much, tell me and I'll stop."

"You said you were married. Is this the reason it didn't work out, Dane? Did he get overloaded and leave you?"

"Something like that. I'm an empath and a telepath. I know you understand what those are, but I want to explain how they affect me. I can feel your emotions and the more of a person I can touch without a barrier, the stronger the feelings are. When Nathan and I married, I tried to explain to him what I could do. He seemed to think he could make me turn it off. I tried, but it got to be too hard during sex. The more I tried to keep my curse from touching him, the more...unfulfilling our sex life became. Then one night, I just let go. He left and filed for divorce the next morning."

"He was an ass. Did he know what you did before you married him? I don't understand why he would marry you and not be more understanding." Jamie was sure there was more, but he didn't ask.

"Thank you, and yes, he knew. He thought he was the man and he would control me and through me, it. We didn't love each other. He needed someone to hang on his arm and I wanted security. We were only married for six weeks. It may have been less if I had listened to Pi in the first place. She has some very colorful words to describe Nathan Wallace."

Jamie was sure she had. He had not known the older woman long, but he knew her to be very blunt and open about her opinion. He decided that he would sit down and have a talk with her soon. He just hoped he did not get a migraine when he did. He started to smile at the thought, but his breath caught when Dane took off her shirt.

"I'm going to sit on you. And it's important that you listen to me, James. When you've had enough, tell me and I'll stop. You'll understand why I need to stop this before it gets too far between us. You're a very nice man, but I don't need anyone. All right?"

"Show me, Dane. I want to know you, all of you." He wanted to tell her it was too late to stop anything between them now. Not when he just realized that he didn't want to, no, he couldn't lose her.

She slipped her pants off and stood before him in her panties and bra. His cock ached and he wondered if he would be able to stand too much of her touching him before he came in his pants like a teenager. When she moved up over his stomach and straddled him, he could not help reaching up and running his hands up her thighs.

"Lie still and don't touch me. Not until I tell you to and then only as I instruct you. This is important, James. Please?"

"All right, baby. I'll behave, but I want you to know that I'm as hard as stone and want you in the worst way. My cock is hurting now."

"Close your eyes." He did so immediately. When she didn't move, he peeked at her. "You didn't hesitate. You just closed them."

Sitting up with her on his hips now, he kissed her. It was quick and hot, full of need and promise. Then he lay back down and closed his eyes. "I trust you, that's why."

"I'm going to run my hands over your ribs and let some of me go. Tell me what you feel." Her finger tips were cool against his warm skin and he felt his muscles ripple with pleasure. When he started to tell her how erotic it felt, he felt the first touch of unease.

"It's mine not yours. I'm not comfortable with touching you like this, bare skin to bare skin. The uncertainty you are feeling is mine. Let it flow through you, touch you."

As her fingers continued to move, he concentrated. "You're more confident now. I can feel it, can't I?"

"Yes. I'm going to give you a little more. Not much, but a little more. This room is white because, as you've guessed, it's my paradisiacal retreat. No one has ever been in here, not even Pi. I don't bring work in here. There are no books to read, no computers, and no sound once the door is closed. What are you feeling, James?"

"You're relaxed. I can feel your need too. You're scared, aren't you, Dane? You're afraid that I'm going to reject you and you're holding yourself back from me. You don't want to go to the next step because you want me to like you."

"I...yes. That's right. You're doing well. I'm going to put my hands on you now and open more. You'll be able to read my thoughts, my emotions through our connection because I'm letting you. I can read yours too."

Her hands opened over his chest and he felt a surge of heat from them. It took his breath away when she leaned down and licked at his nipple then nipped at it. He raised his hand to pull her to his mouth, but she pressed it back to the bed.

The first thing he felt was her need. Sharp and hot. He let himself open to her and was nearly overwhelmed with the flood of things that hit him. He almost cried out when the pain of her back touched him. Pain ripped through her in an instant. Her murmured voice calmed him as more and more touched him.

"James, touch my legs with your fingertips. Don't move them, just touch me. Let the heat build until you can't take it anymore then pull away."

Her voice was hypnotic and soothing. Lifting his hands, he barely touched her thigh when she moaned. This time, there were clips of images. They were not long enough to make out, but her voice told him that he could control them through her, slow them if he wanted or skip them altogether.

Dane, he was seeing these things through Dane's point of view. She looked at a woman, Pi, as she cried, sobbed, and he could feel the pain of Dane's sorrow. A death of a child, Pi's child. Dane had helped Pi find her. An older woman who looked at Dane with love and understanding, hope and sorrow. Her grandmother was like her. Dane's gift was from her.

"That's right, my grandmother knew I was different and had offered to raise me, but my parents didn't want to be shamed by giving up on me. I'm stronger than Grandmother. Her gift was just empathic and telepathic. I'm also clairvoyant too. James, have you had enough yet?"

Had he? He didn't think he would ever get enough of this woman. Her touch ignited him and set him aflame. Her voice caressed him and sent shivers along his spine in ways he'd never felt before. He loved her. Just as simple as that, Jamie realized he was in love with Dane.

Chapter 9

Dane felt the moment he thought of love and tried to pull away from his touch. He grabbed her legs and sat up. His mouth covered her immediately and she knew he would not leave her now. Wrapping her arms around his neck, she leaned into his body, into his heat and love.

"I don't want to hurt you. I will, but I don't want to. Please take me, James. Please have sex with me."

"No, Dane, I'm going to make love to you. Open yourself to me, baby. I want all of you. Give it all to me."

She watched as his hands skimmed along her legs and up her ribs. When he lifted her breasts up and pushed them together, she moaned deep in her throat. Her nipples puckered tight and ached for his mouth. Reaching between his hands, she unsnapped the tiny clasp and pulled her bra open for him. His mouth, hot and wet, took her breast into him and he bit her before she was able to pull her bra off her body. Shifting a little, Dane wrapped her legs around his waist and pulled her lower body tight against his as he suckled and tormented her breasts. His cock was hard against her and she wanted more of him.

Bracing her hands on his shoulders then down around his waist, she began to ride him. She surged her body on his cloth-covered cock as he tasted one then the other breast, going back and forth between them over and over. When he flipped her to her back and came down on her, she came. It was hard and quick and only made her more needy, more achy for him.

"That's it, baby. Don't hold back. Come when you feel it. Come and scream for me. I love to watch you peak. Your body shudders over mine, and I feel you. Feel you everywhere."

He moved down her body. When he forced her legs to let him go, she whimpered and tried to pull him back, but he kissed her hard and brought his hand to her mound.

"I'm going to eat you here, Dane. I'm going to lick you and taste you until you can't stand it anymore. I'm going to drink you as you come, as you fill me. Then I'm going to drive my cock hard into you. Deep and fast and fuck you until neither of us can move."

When he moved this time, she grabbed the sheet beneath her. She could feel her pussy flutter and gush. Need curled inside of her and she had a hard time holding the part of her back that terrified her more than anything.

Jamie nuzzled her mound and when she felt him move the bit of lace from her, she tried to close her legs to him. He pressed her open and braced her with his shoulders as he ran his finger along her slit, gathering her cream as he went.

"Watch me, Dane. I want you to see me lick your cream from my fingers." He brought his fingers to his mouth and suckled each one, savoring the taste. "Hummm, you taste better than I thought, baby. Like honey and peaches."

When his finger slid into her, she could not stop watching him, seeing the look of rapture on his face. Struggling now to hold on, she knew she was slipping. More of her was getting away from her and he knew it.

"I want you, Dane. All of you. Please, baby, trust me."

He pumped his finger into her over and over and when he added a second one, he lowered his head and slid his tongue into her. Moving more between her legs, he worried her clit with his tongue as he fucked her with his fingers. The coil of need tightened around her so tight she tried again to pull back.

Every time she got close, he would pull back and not touch her clit until the need to come lowered a bit. But it was getting harder and longer to slow down. Wrapping her hand into his hair, she tried to get him to where she wanted, but he was stronger and did what he wanted. Begging only made him chuckle and when she thought she was going to have to hurt him, he gave her what she wanted.

He bit her clit hard and then suckled it into his mouth as he'd done her nipples; she knew it was too much. Her control snapped and so did her hold.

Her world froze for a second then everything in her shattered. She knew she screamed. It ripped from her throat, leaving it raw and sore. Every nerve, every cell in her body exploded. Stars, bright and colorful, burst behind her closed eyes. Muscles contracted, her body expanded, and when she felt Jamie move over her and his cock slide into her, she screamed again. Her body tightened around him, pulling his cock deeper into her. Dane heard him growl, heard him speak, but she was beyond knowing what he said. As soon as he was close enough to touch, she wrapped around him and let go.

~~~

Her love poured into him, her climax rippled through him. He felt it along his cock, but also along his heart and mind. He felt her try to pull back, but he rocked into her again and felt her again. Her terror, her needs, he felt her shame and her feelings of failure. It was nearly overwhelming, nearly consumed him, but he loved her and with that knowledge, Jamie knew that she was just what she said. He not only believed her in that moment, but he believed in her.

Watching her face, seeing her emotions fly across it, his climax gripped him in surprise. It grabbed him tight around his cock and poured from him, his seed pouring into her, filling her body with his. When she came again, pulled hard at his cock, he surged again, his body spent but needing to be deep within her. When he could not move anymore, he dropped over her and rolled. He was just able to pull her body over his and lean down for the blanket before sleep took him. Pulling her tight against him, he told her he loved her and fell into an exhausted, sated sleep.

When Jamie woke up, the room was dark and he was alone in the bed. He started to get up, but heard the door open and saw Dane come into the room and go to the window seat he did not notice before. She sat there and looked out at the moonlight. He propped his head up with the two pillows, leaned back against the headboard, and waited.

"I've never come like that before. Well, that's an understatement. I've never come at all if that's what it's like to come with someone." He wanted to get up and do a happy dance at her confession, but was afraid he did not have enough strength in his legs for it.

"Neither have I. I didn't think it was possible to feel that much with another being before. Are you all right?" Jamie asked her.

"Yes. No. I don't...I couldn't hold it back. I tried, but it was...you took my breath away."

"Come here, Dane. I need to hold you." He waited for her to move and when she did not, he started to go to her. He stopped when she started to speak.

"When I was a little girl, about six, there was this girl who lived next door. I could feel her pain, but it frightened me. One day, I saw her in the back yard. She was huddled around a dolly. It was battered and torn, though it was in better shape than the girl. Brenna Print was her name.

"I walked over to her and sat next to her on the snowy ground. I knew my mother was going to have a fit because I was sitting in the dirt, but more so because I was associating with the 'white trash' next door. My grandmother was coming, you see. And everything had to be perfect.

"Neither of us said a word and I'm not sure how long we even sat there, but eventually, Brenna reached out and touched my hand. My little body rocked with her pain. Her injuries were massive and harsh. Her father beat her for anything and everything. He blamed her for her mother leaving and for his lack of work. He hurt her because the cable was out and he hated her for her inability to do anything right."

When she didn't say anything for several minutes, Jamie got up and sat behind her on the seat. There was a throw near them so he picked it up and pulled it over them both as she leaned back against him. Her pain moved along his skin as though it was his and he pulled her tighter to him.

"When her daddy came out, I stood up and shielded Brenna from him. I'm not sure what I could have done against a grown man, but I stood there and waited for him to come at us, or her. He shouted for her to come inside, but neither of us moved. I heard my grandmother's car pull up and I felt her touch me, her mind touch mine. Before I knew it, she was standing in the yard with me and yelling at the man to back off. She had her driver call the police and we stood there together and waited. When they arrived, Brenna was taken to the hospital and the man was arrested."

"There's more, isn't there? Tell me, baby. What did your mother do to you?"

"It was the first time she beat me. My grandmother begged her to let me go live with her before she left. I remember them arguing about someone teaching me to use my gifts and my mother telling her that she knew how to teach me. I was actually excited to learn. That night, she drugged me. I don't know what she used, but it knocked me out. When I woke, I was tied to a beam in the basement. I was gagged and standing on a crate. She had taken my clothes off me and stood there waiting for me to wake. I was hit thirty-one times that night. It may have been more, but I passed out."

Jamie did not say anything. He wasn't sure what to say. He knew from Cait that her mother would beat her. He just didn't know how much.

"My mother went to the police and told them I had mental problems. She told them that I had more than likely hurt Brenna to make people notice me and that they shouldn't believe a word that came out of my mouth. Brenna was released to her father again while I still hung in the basement. By the time I was able to move again, her father had killed her and buried her in the back yard. I told my mother what had happened and she told me 'good riddance,' that one less welfare brat in the world was fine by her. I never spoke to her again until the day I asked for her help with the murders when I was sixteen."

Jamie tried to imagine not speaking to his mother for ten years and couldn't even fathom not speaking to her for ten days. She was his world, his rock and his foundation. He pulled Dane deeper under his chin and held her.

He was so lost in thought that he didn't even know that she had fallen asleep until she snored softly against his shoulder when she turned. Sliding out from under her, he picked her up and put her into the bed. He looked at his watch and saw that it was just after three in the morning. He had a class in less than five hours. He didn't know what to do. Setting his phone to wake him, he crawled into bed again and was rewarded with Dane curling around him. He was asleep in seconds, warm and held tightly.

Chapter 10

Dane was alone when she woke this time. There was a note on the pillow next to her and she picked it up to read it.

"*Love,*

If I could have, I'd have stayed and made love to you all morning. But I have class until three today. Call me when you get up and if I don't answer, leave me a number to call you. I love you, Dane.

James"

The words of love frightened her a bit and she tried not to think about them as she showered and dressed. Her body was sore in places, but she felt more relaxed than she had in months, maybe even years. Pi was in the kitchen when she came downstairs.

"Land owner called. He said tell you we have thirty days. I tell him we need more, but he said no. I have houses marked to look at, Missy Dane. You go with me today? We have to make decision."

"I thought we were going back home, Pi. Isn't that what you want anymore? We can just put this stuff in storage, or sell it. It wasn't anything we'd grown attached to much anyway, was it?"

"You leave man who love you? You be stupid to do that, Missy Dane. Man don't come along much who care for you like Mister Jamie does. You stay and make babies with him. He take care of you."

"Men will say anything to get into a woman's bed, Pi. You know that. He doesn't love me. How could he? My own mother didn't. I'll sleep with him, but that's all. If you want to go look at houses today, we will, but no more talk about love."

Pi was just about to impart some snarky remark, Dane was sure, when the phone rang. Dane wanted to ask her not to answer it and Pi even waited to see if she would, but Dane knew it didn't matter. She would just have to check the voice mail and call Markus back anyway.

"Missy Dane, please take time off. You get sick again. I don't want to have you sick. You my friend."

"You're mine too. I love you, Pi, but he needs me and I have to help. Please answer for me."

Markus needed her in Nevada this time. There was a missing woman and her son and the husband was frantic with worry.

"Why can't you just send the stuff here again? I'm too tired to leave again. Just send it here and I'll let you know if I find anything. I'm worn out, Markus."

"You're not quitting on me are you, Dane? That doesn't sound like you. Come on, just this one and I promise to give you as much time as you need to rest up. I need you here because this is where she went missing. Please?"

"Markus, that's what you said the last time, and the time before that. I can't keep doing this. I need some time off. I appreciate you keeping me out of the media, but I'm exhausted and I need to have some down time. I'm not getting sick like before."

Anger surged through the phone at her. Anger and something that was there and gone so quickly that she nearly missed it. Hate—white-hot hate that boiled over her and through her. Fear rippled through her. Then he was talking again.

"You come out here and fix this for us and I'll make sure I don't call you for a while. You're right, I've been pushing you pretty hard, but you're needed so much that I forget about you sometimes. Please come out and I'll make it right."

Dane looked at Pi. Dane was missing something and she was not sure what it was. When she tried again to read Markus, she hit a wall. If it was from the distance or the phone, she didn't know, but she did not want to go to Nevada. Not now, not ever.

"Let me think about it. I'll call you back tonight and I'll give you my answer then. I have to go house hunting and we were just about to walk out the door. I promise I'll give it my utmost consideration. Good bye, Markus." Without waiting for him to reply, she hung up. She turned to Pi.

"What is it, Missy Dane? He say something bad to you? I hurt his twig and berries this time for sure. He never get it up again."

"No, nothing like…twig and berries? I don't even want to know. Let's get going. I have to leave a number for James, but all I have is this one. Why don't we stop at the mall and get us a cell phone for ourselves? I want one that you can watch programs on. How about it?"

Dane went to her room and got dressed. She did not look at the bed that smelled like James. She had already used the towel that he had when she got out of the shower. Feeling incredibly stupid for acting like a love sick teenager, she dropped it into the hamper, but not before putting it to her nose and smelling for his scent again.

The first stop was lunch. It was nearly eleven and both women were starved. Dane wanted to try something different, like anything that was not Chinese, and Pi agreed just this once she would go along. They had an enjoyable lunch of pasta and salad and Pi had two shots of Saki. It made for an interesting early afternoon.

The phone buying was funny and by the time they were given their new numbers and shown how to use them, it was nearly two. Dane called Jamie's office and left her new number for him, telling him that she and Pi were out and that she did not know when they would be back. If he wanted to meet them for dinner somewhere, that would be fine too.

They were looking at the second house when he called her back. Pi had already crossed the first one off the list and this one was not fairing much better. Something was wrong with them both and no amount of trying to tell her that it could be changed helped. When Dane answered, she was a little tense.

"Having a bad day? You sounded so happy earlier. What's happened?" She could just picture him sitting at a desk with his feet propped up.

"Pi doesn't like this house because the kitchen is too small. Just how big does a kitchen have to be anyway? It's to cook in, not raise a family in. The last house didn't have a yard. Okay, I agree with that one. I need to build something on the property and that was a little yard." She took a deep breath and forced a smile in her voice. "How's your day going?"

"I wanted to stay in bed with this beautiful woman, but duty called and I had to leave. I have an idea, why don't the two of you come over to my house for dinner? I have a huge kitchen and Byron and Taylor are coming over too. I was thinking Pi could fix us some more of that Kung Pao that we had the other day at your townhouse. And Morgan wants to be there too. You think that would be all right? Or we can go out. It's up to you guys."

Dane turned to Pi and asked her. To be honest, Dane didn't want to go home anyway. She'd have to deal with Markus and she hadn't thought of him as much as she thought she might. It was too nice being normal for a change. Dane handed her phone to Pi when she started asking questions about the cooking arrangements.

She needed to make things right with Cait, Dane knew that. She had thought about the way she had treated the woman all these years after talking with Jamie. It was not fair what she had done, or what she had said to her. When Pi handed her the phone, Dane made a decision.

"Do you think your entire family would like Pi's cooking? I mean, if she's going to cook for a bunch of people, everyone might as well enjoy it, don't you think? Unless you'd rather they didn't. I can understand that." She closed her eyes and hoped he would understand what she was asking.

"I'm sure they would. Cait and Spencer won't be able to make it. She's still in the hospital, but I think Paddy gets to go to the nursery tomorrow. Maybe someone can take her some leftovers, if there are any."

Dane took at deep breath. "No. Pi loves to cook. I just hope your kitchen is big enough. She can get quite messy when cooking. We'll clean up before we leave so don't worry about that."

"I'm not worried, because you're not leaving. I plan on making love to you again all night and in my bed.

Tomorrow's Saturday, I don't have to get up early, and you are not going to be able to move."

"Oh." She felt stupid, but that's all she could squeak out. Her body felt as if he was standing next to her breathing on her neck, his fingers caressing her skin.

"Oh is right. I'll see you at six. I love you, Dane." And then he was gone.

Dane and Pi ended up at the grocery store next. Neither of them wanted to look at any more houses and they had already set up three appointments for tomorrow afternoon and three more for Sunday.

~~~

Jamie was headed out the door at five-thirty when his phone rang again. He did not recognize the number so was slightly cautious when he answered. But the frantic-sounding foreign language at the other end threw him.

"Missy Dane break car bad. She call a-team now. You have swirl or gas to use at house?"

Jamie sat down. "Pi?" He was trying to work out what she said when his office phone rang too. It was Damon. He answered it as well. "Hang on, I got another call."

"Yes, it Pi. You know more Chinese women? I say Missy Dane break car. You have gas?"

"Dane wrecked the car. Is she all right? Where are you?" Jamie stood and almost strangled himself with the other phone.

"She call a-team now. You very hard to understand. You don't speak good English." Jamie was not even going to go there. He felt as if he was in an off world and he was the only one speaking his language.

Damon said, "Triple A, maybe? Ask if she called an ambulance. I haven't a clue on the gas, buddy."

"Dane called Triple A? Is there an ambulance on the way?" Jamie started rubbing his forehead. He wanted to hang up with his brother and go to Dane, but he was afraid he'd need him to translate again.

"That what I said." More Chinese, then he heard Dane. "She mad at me. Said I should mind own business. I ask you who business is it when man try to kill us both? You come and get us? We at Asian Market at Three Z's road. Missy Dane head hurt, but she be fine she said."

"I'll meet you at your house. I was just calling to confirm. Should I tell the others to not come?" Damon was saying. Jamie was sure he should say no, but knew that he needed to make sure Dane got to his house. Without Pi there, he knew that Dane would not come either.

"No. You can look at her there. Christ, I have a headache. I'll pick them up and bring them to the house. Could you call Tucker for me and have him meet me at the Asian market on Triple C? I'm sure that's where they are."

It took him less than twenty minutes to get there and Tucker was already there. He was rubbing his forehead as he stood in front of Pi. The woman was gesturing at ninety miles a minute. Jamie knew just how he felt. He saw Dane sitting in the back of an ambulance with her head between her knees. When she sat up to look at the medic standing outside the open doors, his heart clenched in his chest. Her face was bloodied and she had been crying.

Chapter 11

Dane saw him coming toward her and wanted to leap from the bed and go to him. Her head was pounding, but she was not sure if it was from all the noise and people or her hitting her head on the steering wheel. She also did not know if she was mad at him or not. But when he touched her arm and then pulled her into his, she melted against him and started crying. He didn't say anything. He just held her.

"Are you all right, baby? Pi was a little…well, I was going to say hard to understand, but I think you know what I mean. I'm either going to have to get a translator or learn Chinese. I still have no idea what she meant by my indigestion."

"Indigestion? I'm afraid I don't know either. I told her not to call anyone. The guy must not have had insurance so he didn't hang around. They've taken away our car. I don't know how I can…I can't ride in a taxi everywhere I go."

"We'll figure it out. My brother is going to meet us at my house since you won't go to the hospital. We'll figure out what she meant about swirling or gas. I cannot imagine what she wanted to know for."

"Oh. Gas or electric. What do you cook with, gas or electric?" Dane watched the police captain come toward her. She might have laughed at his expression if she could not feel him so loudly. He was being promoted but was afraid he would mess up the job so badly he'd be fired, or someone would get hurt.

"Your friend said that you were stopped when you were hit. That sound about right, Mrs. Wallace? She gave me a description of the car, but...well, could you maybe help me out? I think there might have been a bit of a...language barrier. Plus, I'm not so sure she thinks I'm going to do a damned thing about this."

"We were stopped at the sign there at the end of the street. The black SUV ran the light and hit us. He probably didn't have insurance or something. I think...Pi was in the back seat or she might have been seriously hurt. I'm sure it's all right, Captain."

"Well, ma'am, I might believe that if I didn't already have a few questions about the night Mr. Grant here was beat up in the park. I know you said you weren't doing anything illegal, but now this is the second attempt on your life in about a week. Next time you might not be so lucky."

"This was a simple case of hit and run. I don't know how you'd think it was anything but. Pi didn't say that, did she? I think she watches too many police shows." Dane looked around, suddenly scared.

The car that had followed her the other night had been a dark SUV. The night that Jamie had been attacked, there had been another one parked next to her car. She swayed slightly and had it not been for Jamie, she would have fallen.

"Wanna start from the top again? What can you tell me about the car, Mrs. Wallace? Did you see a plate number? Anything that might make it stand out to you?" Captain Tucker's voice sounded tense and she was having a hard time focusing on it.

She stood and without looking at either man, she pulled out her phone. "I'll call us a taxi to take us home."

When Jamie took the phone from her and closed it, she started to demand it back, but the look in his eyes stopped her. He looked not angry, but very angry. She started to turn away from him and was surprised when he pulled her against his body.

"Tuck, I'm taking the women home to my house. My family is waiting on us. Damon will have a look at her head. If you wouldn't mind stopping out there after you're done here, that'd be great. I don't think she should be out like this much more, do you?"

Dane was sure that the cop wanted to disagree, but he too must have seen something in the younger man's eyes and agreed to come by later. Jamie did not so much as lead her to his car, but dragged her behind him in a long stride she had to run to keep up with.

"I really don't think —" He turned back so quickly she ran into him. She backed up as far as she could with him still holding her hand.

"Not a word. I mean it, Dane. You say one word and I will haul you over my lap and beat your ass." When she opened her mouth, he took a step toward her and she snapped it closed again.

Their groceries were loaded into his car and they were on the way within ten minutes. He still had not said a word and for once, Dane was glad that Pi did not shut up. But as each mile passed, Dane got madder herself. By the time they pulled into his driveway, she was boiling over.

The door opened as she walked up the steps and Dane went inside, past the three people sitting in the living room, and straight to the bathroom. She was going to be sick.

Nothing churned her belly up like anger, and she had plenty of it.

"Open the damned door. I want to talk to you. Dane, damn it, I said to open the fucking door."

She threw open the door and right at him. "Now you want to talk! Now you have something to say to me? You ever treat me like I'm some five-year-old again and I will knock you on your ass. The nerve of you telling me that you will beat my ass like I'm...I'm not a child, do you hear me! Having sex with you does not mean you have the right to act like I'm some...some possession of yours. That man wants me dead. Dead, did you hear me?"

"Were you going to tell me that you were being followed? Did it occur to you that you might be in danger and that I'd, gee, I don't know, maybe might care? Did you even think that..."

"Of course, I forgot to include the great James Andrew Grant in my daily musings. Let me see, today I thought about buying a house and believe it or not, I made the decision to have red sauce instead of white on my pasta, and eight days ago before I had sex with you, a man followed me home. Pardon me all to hell and back because I didn't think to let you know then. Would you also like to know that I plan to take a shower later? In my own home, in my own apartment?"

"You are not going anywhere. That man wants you dead and in the event that you may have missed it, I love you. And it's my right to keep you—"

Dane never hit. And she seldom let herself get so angry that she thought about it, but he just set her over the edge. Drawing back her small fist, she hit him right in the nose. When he staggered back and fell against the wall across from her, she turned, went down the hall and out the sliding glass door into the back yard, and screamed.

~~~

Damon helped him up and he started for the sliding door to follow Dane when Nick stepped in front of him. "I wouldn't if I were you. Let's go into the kitchen and have a beer. Morgan and Taylor can handle it for now."

"I'm not through talking to her. Move, Nicky, or I swear I'll hurt you. She could have been killed today and—"

"Yeah, we all heard. And I think she knows that more than you. If you actually love this woman like you said, then I'd give her some space right now. Besides, I think she might have broken your nose. Let Damon look at it. She fights pretty well for a girl. Didn't see that punch coming, did you?"

Jamie looked at the door Dane had gone out and saw his two sisters-in-law out there with her. He knew that if he went out now they'd just argue more and then maybe one or all three of the women would beat up on him too. Jamie went to the kitchen where his brothers were. Pi was at the stove, quiet for once.

His nose was not broken, but he was going to have a black eye. Byron would not stop laughing and as soon as his mother came in the house, he retold the entire story to her—including the curse words. She tsked at him and went out to the back yard too. Captain Tucker and Spencer showed up ten minutes later.

"Cait wants me to ask her some questions too. And I'm supposed to tell you that there had better be leftovers or she's going to make sure you get a ticket every time you leave the house. What happened to your nose?"

"She's in the back with the other women plotting his demise, I bet. Dane hit him. It was the best thing I've seen in a long time. She just came out of the bathroom and socked him one." Byron started again.

"Yeah, like the time Taylor knocked your nuts up around your ears? That was good too. Leave off, ass, or you won't get any dinner either." Jamie was starting to realize that he might have been just a little too strong with Dane and that maybe, just maybe, he deserved to be hit. Of course he had no plans of telling these idiots that, but he planned to tell Dane. If she let him.

When the women came in a few minutes later, he stood up and met her at the door. She would not look at him and he cupped the back of her head and kissed her. At first, he didn't think she was going to respond, but when she did, he thought he might be all right.

"I'm not your possession, you understand me? And I won't be talked to like I'm five years old. I get followed a lot. Newspaper reporters, other families who think I can help them. They want a story and I like my privacy. I'm sorry I didn't tell you, but—"

He kissed her again, deeper this time, and when she leaned into him, Jamie wanted to tell his family to go away, but was also glad for their support.

"I'm an ass and I'm sorry. I love you. I know you find that hard to believe right now, but I do. I'll try not to act like an idiot too much when we're together."

They went into the kitchen again just in time to hear his mother talking about the food Pi was serving up.

"...fat as a house if I did. My goodness, Pi. This is delicious. You should open a restaurant. I'll be there every day. Wait until I tell Cait. Hello, Dane, honey. You feeling better? You have color in your cheeks again." Jamie glared at Byron when he laughed.

"Yes, ma'am. I'm sorry about the outburst. Some people need to learn their boundaries. When Pi and I went by the house to get her wok, I picked up something for you and something for someone to take to the new baby. I also have a few gifts for the other children as well. Pi and I don't get to shop…I'm not much of a shopper."

Dane went over to one of the many bags he'd brought in and she began pulling things out. He was surprised at the amount of things that there were and was just walking over to help when she stood up. She handed his mother a shoe box and then passed out things to the other children.

She gave Meggie a hand held game. "I'm not sure if you have one or not, but the clerk said that you'd have fun with it. Jamie, could you tell her I'm sorry, but I don't know sign language yet?"

"She said that she doesn't have this one here, that her mother wouldn't let her have it when she came to live with Spence and Cait." Spencer signed his reply to them both for her. "She said to tell you thanks and she'll be more than glad to teach you sign language. She said she's already teaching Ronnie and you can join in."

"Oh, that would be great. This is for the boys. I know they aren't children, but I wanted to get them something too. Someone can take them back to the mall so they can spend it, right? I don't listen to music myself so I wasn't sure what to…Jamie?"

He went to her, took the bag, and finished handing out the gifts. Morgan and the twins were opening theirs when he finished. When one of the twins hugged her, Jamie nearly went to pull him away when Pi stopped him.

"Babies don't hurt. She say they got no hurts yet and they don't hurt her. I need talk to you, Mister Jamie. Later. I have much to say."

Jamie nodded and wondered what she could possibly say to him and if he would understand her when she did. Then she announced that dinner would be in ten minutes. He did not know what else she could have. They had all been eating since they got there.

"Now, that's just enough time for me to see what we have here. Come sit beside me, Dane. I want to see what you've brought this old woman."

Margaret took off the lid and when she drew in a deep breath, Jamie leaned over to see what it was. Pictures. Lots of them too. They were in a filelike order with dates along the tabs and the picture in a neat order.

"They're my grandmother's pictures. I've made you copies of those. I don't know some of the places, but you're in most of them in the front. I think the older man is your husband. There are even a few of your oldest sons. If you don't want them, that's okay. You probably have most of them anyway."

"Oh Dane, these are wonderful. This is my husband when we were dating. Look, Byron, it's your grandfather here with your dad. And look, the oldest, Spencer. Oh, Spencer, you'll love this for your new son. I'm going to have these framed. Won't they look wonderful with the ones in the den? Dane, honey, this is the best...I don't know what to say."

"I found them among my grandmother's things when she passed away. She had so many pictures that I'm having them put into albums. There are quite a few tintypes too. Those are the only ones that I've had a chance to go through. It hurt to...some of them still have...well, I can't touch them anymore. I had to have someone do it for me."

Pi called them to the dinner table with a promise that she would tell them what they were being served. The table was huge, but not near big enough for them all. The adults sat at the table and the children crowed around in chairs from the kitchen.

They'd already eaten some pretty amazing dishes as she went about cooking the main course. There had been egg rolls and dumplings as well as something she called satay chicken. She said that it was actually a Thai recipe, but she really liked it. As each dish was served around the table, she told them what it was.

"That Kung Pao chicken that Mister Jamie asked for. I make with no veggie. Some people don't like. That Moo Goo Gai Pan, Missy Dane favorite. I make extra sauce to cover rice. Vegetables are on side, but I make lots. Need to keep strength up. Some don't like rice, but I have no time to make noodles so these bought. They be okay, but not fresh. Missy Dane like noodle with snap pea and she like almond cookies. I make them next time."

The dinner was great. And as soon as it was over, Captain Tucker, Spencer, Devin, and Dane met in the study. Dane was nervous and Jamie knew that he would be as well if it were him.

Chapter 12

Dane sat in one of the chairs. Jamie had told her that he wanted to talk to Byron, but he would be in shortly. She did not want to be here, but she knew that they had questions and she was the only one who could answer them.

"Mrs. Wallace, I know that you—"

"I'm sorry, Captain Tucker. I'm Doctor Danish Messenger Wallace. If you want to call me anything, please call me Dane. I'm no longer married, and only use the Wallace part when I'm trying to keep my personal life separate from my business one. And after today, I'm pretty sure you understand why I like to remain as far away as possible when it comes to the media and the police."

"Yes, ma'am. O'Malley explained to me that you're a tad unique. She said to tell you if I fucked this up—pardon, ma'am, her words not mine, that she'd kick my...well, O'Malley has a colorful vocabulary when it suits her. She didn't explain too much, only said you'd tell me something that I might find hard to believe, but that you were trustworthy."

"I don't trust anyone much, especially those I just met. You be honest with me and I'll be honest with you. I'm not going to go into detail that you don't need, but I've had problems with the police before in the States. I've only just moved back here since my grandmother died and I was trying to make a fresh start. I've been followed before, not so much in China, but a few times I've come back to visit. The hit today was a surprise. I'm not sure what I can help you with concerning it."

"Do you think that you were the target at the Quad? I mean, in light of what happened today, could you instead of Jamie have been the one they were been after in the first place?" Tucker pulled out his note pad as he asked.

Dane looked around the room. Two men she barely knew and she did not know if she could trust them. Devin hadn't done anything but be honest with her and Captain Tucker didn't seem to have any ill will toward her, but who knew what he would tell her just to make a quick buck. She got up to pace the room and that's when Jamie walked in.

"Captain Tucker, before I answer that may I ask you a question? And I'll know if you're lying to me. The little boy who was killed by his mother, where do the police think you got that information? I know that Mr. Grant here told you that I'm the source, but what do your men know?"

"All right. I can see where you're going. My men don't give two rats' asses where the information came from. We got his killer and we were able to bury him. Not many times can we say that when it comes to kids nowadays. I told them we had a tip, it paid off, and we're happy. You tell me how you knew, well, missy, I'm gonna believe you the best I can. If you're asking me if I'll tell anyone, then nope. You play in my sandbox." He winked at her. "And so long as the cat don't piss in it, we'll be all right together. Pardon my language."

Dane couldn't help it, she burst out laughing. She thought it was the wink, but it could also have been the sandbox story. She decided she liked this man.

"I'm a telepath and an empath. I can't read thoughts like they show you on the television, but I can get images, scents, and sometimes little snippets of movielike information. It's not always enough, but it helps me narrow things down. The other night when you came to the apartment, I'd been searching for the missing boys. Though the boy had never worn it, his mother had touched the shirt. From there I was able to see what she had done."

"Just from touching the shirt?" Spencer asked her.

"I'm a clairvoyant too. I can touch things that have been touched with a great deal of emotion tied to them. For example, this picture." Dane tipped the picture over to its face, but didn't look at it. "I know that a man put this in the frame. He had a cut on his index finger that was hurting him at the time and he was angry at his child. No, not at the child but for it—a male. They had been...playing with paper, an airplane, and his son had been hurt. A tree, the plane is there. And a trip to the hospital, and there is pride there as well."

Devin walked over and picked up the framed picture Dane had turned over and looked at it. His smile was radiant. He turned to the policeman.

"It's the day Byron fell from the apple tree getting the paper plane Dad and he had made together. Mom has never let him forget that he walked to the hospital when he'd fallen rather than come home so she could take him. Dad had tried to be stern with Byron, but he couldn't be. He told him that a real man knows when the shortest distances between needing your mom and knowing to get help is pride. Dad had been very proud of Byr that day."

"I know that James was the intended target that day because I can't read me. Whenever anything happens to me, it's just as much a surprise to me as it is to anyone else." She sat down as she continued. "I'd had dreams about James and he was supposed to die that night. He was going to be stabbed to death and bleed out before anyone found him the next morning. I don't remember touching those men, or James, but at some point, I had. I had to save him and it was within my power to do so."

Devin handed her the picture and their fingers touched. She jerked back and the picture would have fallen to the floor, but he grabbed for it and caught it. When she stood back up and Devin looked at her, Dane looked at Jamie.

"It was him. They weren't looking for you to die, but Devin. The connection is there. They were looking for your brother."

"Dane, sit down. Tell me what you're talking about. Who wants Devin to die and why?" Jamie pushed her into the chair that Devin had been in and the connection to him got stronger.

"You know the man who attacked Jamie," she said to Devin. "He thought he was after someone else. I didn't understand then, but now that I feel the similarities, I know that they were after you and not Jamie. You know the man who was there."

"Do you know who he is? Or something we can use to get him? I don't know anyone who would want to kill me. Well, my wife most days, but I don't think she'd have me killed over not picking up milk on the way home from work." The laugh was forced.

Dane could feel Devin's nervousness. He was tense and trying to make light of it. She was also surprised at the ease in which he believed her. Dane decided that she'd repay him by helping.

"No, I don't know anything. I can...if you'll trust me, I'll help you sort it out and find him. I won't hurt you, but it will tire you out. But you'd have to trust me." She wanted to say no, but she really wanted to help.

"Tell me what you need. I don't want anyone else in my family to be hurt because of me. Just tell me what you need and I'll do it." Jamie smiled at her encouragingly as Devin finished speaking.

"Just like that. You're going to let me do whatever I need just like that. Why? I mean, how can you know that I won't hurt you, won't harm you in anyway?"

"Because I believe in you and your abilities, more so now than ever. If you say you won't hurt me, then I know you won't. Tell me what you want me to do."

Still shocked, she had him sit in the chair and relax. Dane looked over at the policeman and Jamie. Nerves made her shaky.

"I'm going to read your mind, all of it. When I find the man in your memories, I'll slow them down and let you look at him. If you have any more memories than just his face there, we can dig into those as well. It will exhaust you, but you'll know who he is and the connection to you. Understand?"

"Yes. But how will you feel when this is over? Will you be like you were before, comatose and out of it? I don't want you hurt either. If you can just show me who he is, then that'll be fine."

"I'll need to sleep. I'll...Pi will take care of me. She understands this more than...Just have her take me home and I'll be fine. All right?" She walked behind him and waited. No one said anything so Dane closed her eyes and put her fingers on Devin's head.

~~~

Jamie was not sure what to expect. She simply put her hands on Devin's head and closed her eyes. He kept a close eye on both of them, watching for either of them to be in pain or distress. Devin kept his hands tight on the arms of the chair and a couple of times started to raise them, but Dane would mummer something to him and he'd drop them. Captain Tucker pulled out a recorder and his pen and paper and whenever something was said, he'd make note. About twenty minutes later, Dane said something.

"See that man there, Devin? The one to the left? He's the man who attacked Jamie. You were in the room with him. At some point, he touched you. Shall I move on or do you have enough to find him?"

"I'm sorry, Dane, I don't know anything about him. If you're not too tired, I'd like to move on. He looks somewhat familiar, but not enough to know who he is."

Another fifteen minutes went by when suddenly, Devin stiffened. "You can't pull out yet. We have to move slowly. Take a deep breath and I'll back you out," Dane said to him.

"No! I need to go on. He, I need his name. Can you get it? He...I remember the day, but I need a name."

"If you have it, we'll find it. Shhh...remain calm. When you're tense, I can't move past your block. That's it. Now, see that on the table, did you get close to it, did you touch it? That's it, Devin, move over there and focus. Can you see it?"

"Phillip Sizemore. His name is Phillip Sizemore and the date is February seventeenth. Yes, I know him. I have enough now."

Jamie moved up behind Dane. He could see her swaying slightly and wanted to help her when she came out. His brother slumped in the chair and almost before he could catch her, Dane was out. He held her to his chest and carried her over to the couch. He was pulling a light blanket over her when Donald went to the door to get Damon.

"That is by far the stupidest thing…you could have hurt each other! What the fuck were you thinking? Didn't you learn anything the first time we found her like this? I swear to Christ I should just sedate the both of them and hope they never wake up. Of all the stupid, asinine things to do. I've had—"

"Damon! For Christ's sake, shut the fuck up!" Jamie was worried and it made it hard to control his temper. "They both knew what they were doing. She told him he would be exhausted, but you said yourself they're fine. If you can't be quiet, then leave."

"Jamie, watch your language," Margaret said to him. "And you can take Dane to bed in a moment. Devin, will you be all right for a few minutes? I'd like a word with your brother. Damon, please come with me. The rest of you, sit. If anyone leaves this room before I return, I'll be very displeased."

Jamie held Dane in his arms and stewed. She was not as asleep as she had been, but she was still out. Pi said she didn't sleep long normally and that she would wake soon. She said that she would have a headache for a couple of days, but otherwise be fine. He wanted her awake now and without the headache. He kissed her forehead again.

When his mother and brother came in, Damon looked at Dane then at Devin. Devin walked to his brother and held him. It would be all right between them.

"I'm sorry, Jamie." Damon hugged him too. "I don't want anything to happen to either of them. I don't understand what she can do, but Mom said she's brilliant and that without her she wouldn't have been able to solve the murder of three children. I'm really sorry. I love you guys so much and I don't want—"

"I won't hurt your family, Dr. Grant," Dane said as she sat up. "Never. I'm really tired and if you guys don't mind, I'd like to go home."

"Yeah, about that. There's a slight problem with you going home, Mrs…Dr…Dane." Captain Tucker smiled at them as he continued. "I just got a call from one of my officers and it seems you've had a break in. The place has been trashed and nothing was left untouched. I'm just on my way there now. If you'd like to wait until in the morning, I understand. It'll still be there."

Chapter 13

Dane cried herself to sleep. Jamie walked out into the hall, went to the kitchen to get a beer, and found Pi sitting in the dark. He almost stepped out again to leave her to her quiet when she spoke.

"Missy Dane like my daughter. I love girl so much I hurt when she does. I don't think I can leave her, Mister Jamie. What I do now?"

"What do you mean, Pi?" Jamie sat down across from her as he asked. "Why would you have to leave her? She needs you now more than ever."

"She think no man want her. She say that man who say he love her only want in her bed. I don't think Missy Dane believe that, she just say it to make hurt not so bad. That man she married to, he cruel to her. He try make me stay away and Missy Dane tell him to go to Hades. She tell him that Pi mean more to her than ten of him. He slap her. She hit back and knock him on his butt. He never hit her again."

Jamie burst out laughing at that. Dane had one hell of a punch and decided he'd be more careful in the future. He did not like that Wallace had hit her, but was happy to know that she could stand up for herself.

"I don't think you have to worry about me ever hitting Dane, Pi. I'm in love with her and while I will tell her that to get into her bed, it's not the only reason." He grinned when she did. "But tell me what has you so sad. And why you think you have to leave her. Do you want to return to China?"

"No. I want to be with her. I want to...will you let me have place close to her?" She looked at him with tears in her eyes. "I need Missy Dane and she need me. I won't be problem."

It took Jamie a few seconds to realize what she meant. She was not leaving Dane. She thought he would make her leave Dane. Well, hell. He reached out and took both her hands into his.

"Pi, if you don't want to live here with us too, then I can understand. I had hoped that you knew that you are as welcome here as Dane. She's my life, and with her comes you. I need you to be here for her when I can't. There's plenty of room and if not, then we'll get a bigger house. This house was just something I got as part of the college tenure."

"Missy Dane have big house, but she don't live in it." There was so much hope in Pi's voice. "Her granny leave it to her. It not far from here. She said too big for two people, maybe she sell it. It have big, big kitchen too. It have pool room too to change into white room for her. Missy Dane's granny need quiet room too."

"Pool room?" It took him a second to understand what she meant. "You mean pool house? I understand the white room. Dane said it gives her somewhere to go. Is that what you mean?"

"Yes. Missy Dane get sick again if that man don't let her build it." This time, there was anger, hatred in her voice that he was shocked by. "She tell him lots that she need down time, but he don't listen. He keep pushing her, but she have no room to go to. You tell her not to go to man again. Tell her you need her here for babies."

Babies. He wanted to have babies with Dane. Lots of them. They had not been using any kind of protection and he was almost sorry for that, but he could not help but hope that she would get pregnant with their child. Seeing little Paddy made him ache to see Dane swollen with his child.

"This man, what's his name? And what does he have that makes Dane help him? Does he have some secret that she…has he threatened her?" Something occurred to Jamie. "With exposure. Has he told her if she doesn't help her he'll expose her?"

"Don't know. He is bad man. I don't like him and he know it. I told him I put a hex on his cock so it never rise, but Missy Dane tell me behave. I hope his twig and berries fall off and some little mousey eat them for dinner."

Jamie laughed. She may be difficult to understand at first, but Jamie was getting better and better at figuring her out. He knew that he had to make her know how much he needed her to stay too.

"Pi, we'll both talk to Dane in the morning. Then we're going to discuss where we'll all live. I don't care where it is so long as the three of us are there as a family, all right?"

~~~

It took Dane several minutes to wake up. She started to roll over again and snuggle down into the blankets, but they were too heavy. She tried pulling and tugging, but it would not budge. Finally, she sat up and jerked them.

"All you had to say was, 'James, I'd like more blanket, please.' I don't mind sharing, but to be jerked awake is kind of hard on the system." She was suddenly lying back on the bed. "And speaking of hard…good morning, love."

The kiss was hungry and before she could stop herself, she was feeding him. His mouth could do so much in such a short span of time. When Jamie's tongue slid along hers, she moaned.

"Is there ever a time when you aren't hard? James, we should get...oh my, that feels so good. James, please, I have to go to...I have to go to...somewhere." His chuckle skated along her nipples.

"I need you. And this is the first time I've had you in my bed. So this is as good a time as any to break it in."

She realized she was naked about a second before he took her nipple into his mouth. He sucked at the tip so hard, she knew that she'd come if he kept it up. When she tried to run her fingers into his hair and hold him there, he pulled her arms above her head and held them there.

"You can't touch me. I want to make you so hot that as soon as I touch your pretty pussy, you go off. I plan to take my time this morning and you aren't going to rush me. Just feel me."

He worried her nipples and breasts until she thought she'd scream at him. Then when he started down her ribs and along her belly, Dane wanted to wrap herself around him and hold him tight. His mouth was like a hot blade, sliding along her skin and leaving a trail of heat in its wake. When he whorled his tongue in her belly button and nipped at her there, she nearly came up off the bed.

"You like that, don't you? Hummm, you taste so good. Are you wet for me, Dane? I can smell your heat, your wet heat."

When he slid his fingers into her curls, she tried to close her legs to him. No one had touched her like he did. No one had ever cared if she was wet. James seemed to love it.

"James, please. Just take me. It's hard to hold on when you do that. Please, come inside of me. I need to feel you deep inside."

"I know you like to control, but not when we're in bed. I want you to feel what I'm doing to you. Feel what I'm feeling when I touch you, when I'm tasting you. Center on me, Dane, and what I'm feeling for you."

She tried to block it out, but the more he touched her, the more of his body that touched her, the harder it was for her to pull back. It frightened her, these feeling she had for him. It made her want to pull back more, but he was not letting her.

"James, please. I don't want to hurt you. I just want you to have sex with me. Please, I'm afraid."

"Dane, I'm not going anywhere. I know you can feel this, me touching you. Center on us, focus on us, and I'll catch you."

His fingers were everywhere. His mouth would burn her here and when she regained her hold, he'd be scorching her somewhere else. He'd nip at her hip then her breast. His fingers would slide into her heat and then he'd touch her with his tongue. And always, he was telling her what he felt, how she tasted, how hot her skin was.

It was too much and not enough. She wanted to let go, and she was having a hard time not. Fear of his rejection, fear of hurting him, but mostly she was afraid of what he'd figure out.

"Dane, let go for me. Let me in, baby. Let me have all of you." He suckled her clit as he fucked her with his fingers, two then three of them sliding in and out of her. She was riding his face and his hand, so close that she was aching for it. Then he slid his finger into her tight hole, slid into her ass, and she lost the hold.

His love poured into her, over her, and through her. His touches became more, more heat, more love, more everything. She knew the moment he felt it, the moment that she was feeling him. His smile was like the sun coming out on a cloudy day.

"James, I love you. Please, I need you. I love you."

When he sat up, she whimpered, thinking he was leaving her. He moved to the edge of the bed and looked down at her. Then he stood and removed his boxers. Her mouth watered at the sight of him. His cock was long and thick, the head dark in his need. Reaching up, she smoothed her thumb over the tip to catch the drop of cum there. Taking it to her mouth, she moaned at the taste. It was salty and hot, just like the man. Sitting up, she wrapped her fingers around him and licked him. His hiss had her pulling back.

"I would love to feel you take me into your mouth, but I want to be inside of you in the worst way. Later, later you can have my body and do whatever you want, but now, I want to come inside of you."

Leaning down, he kissed her again. Moving onto the bed, he lifted her legs and put them over his shoulders, lifting her ass up off the bed and giving him the perfect angle to enter her.

"Watch me. I want you to see me move inside of you. Feel me and how good it feels to have you clutching at my cock. I want you to come with me, Dane. I want to feel that tight sheath of yours milk me and pull me deeper into you."

He nudged her entrance and then rocked into her. Opening to him, she felt how hard he was holding back, how he wanted her to come first. Tightening her pelvic muscles, she closed her eyes when he groaned. His control slipped just a little more. She moved again, tightening around him, holding him inside.

"James, come. I want to feel you come. You're so close, let me feel it, please." She begged him, her voice deep with her own need.

Holding her legs high, he moved his free hand down her body and pinched her clit. Rocking harder, his balls slapping against her ass, she felt him stiffen. With a roar, he came. She felt his hot cum splash into her and she came with a scream. Her body bowed up off the bed and he surged harder. Each stroke of his cock sent wave after wave of sensation through her. As soon as her climax started to slow, he'd touch her again, surge into her again, and she'd soar up and over again. When he finally lowered her legs and collapsed on her, she started to slide into a sated sleep. She barely moved when he rolled to his back, taking her with him, did not even register when he pulled the blankets up over them.

Someone was shaking her and she smacked out at them. When the covers suddenly disappeared, she sat up quickly to blast whoever woke her. Jamie stood in front of her with the covers in one hand and a glass of tea in the other.

"Pi said you need a glass of iced tea to wake up. I'll give it to you if you get out of bed. It's freshly brewed and it has a lemon in it." He sipped it and made the most comical face she'd ever seen. "There's no sugar in it. Shit, how do you drink this stuff?"

"I love it. Now hand it over and nobody gets hurt. I need that like a druggie needs a fix. And for as much as I drink of it, the added sugar would make me as big as a house. James, I'm not kidding, give it over."

"No. You get up and kiss me and I'll give you a drink. If you lay there much longer, looking totally delectable, then we'll never leave this room. Pi is about to bust downstairs. I've had to bribe her with all sorts of things to get her to let you sleep this long. It's almost three o'clock. Time's wasting, woman. Up!"

When he walked out of the room with her tea, she yelled at him to come back. When he stood just inside the doorway, she tried to seduce him to the bed by cupping her breasts and trying to look sexy, but he shook his head.

"You've worn me out," Jamie said with a grin. "I might need to have a separate bedroom to keep up with you. Come on, get up and we'll play later."

"James, if you leave the tea on your dresser, I'll have to get—"

He was suddenly on her. His mouth covered hers and invaded her with his tongue. Cupping her breast, he rolled her nipple between his thumb and finger and pinched hard. Pain and pleasure, something she never would have thought to be something she'd enjoy, surged through her body.

"Our dresser. Everything about us is 'ours.' Say it, Dane. You're mine and I belong to you. From this point on, it's 'us,' 'our,' and 'we.' I love you and you love me. Today starts the new us. Understand?"

She looked at him, his eyes dark with need, his cock pressed hard against her body, his hands touching her, soothing her, and she did love him. Reaching up, she ran her fingers through his hair and brushed her lips over his.

"I love you, James. I don't know how you moved into my heart, but I'm glad you did. Ours, yes, I understand. But if you don't give me my tea, I'm going to have Pi put a hex on your twig and berries." He burst out laughing.

After getting out of the shower and having her tea, Dane felt like a new person. She was sore, her body ached in delicious places, and for the first time in a long time, she actually felt rested. She was walking into the bedroom when she realized she had nothing to wear. Going to Jamie's closet, she was just pulling down a shirt of his when Pi walked in.

"Mister Jamie said to bring you clothes. Said that you not run bared butted when we go out. Missy Dane, we go see houses today. We look at granny house too, yes?"

She took the shirt and pants from Pi and sat on the bed. Her granny's house. She'd forgotten about it. Living in the house meant that she'd be taking what had been left to her, all of it.

"We'll look at it." Dane pulled on her pants before continuing. "I don't know if you'll like the kitchen. It's very old. I know Grandmother said she was remodeling, but I don't know what she had done. We'll add it to the list we have today or tomorrow. We have to go by the apartment and see what's there too. I'm sorry about this, Pi. I know we had all of our things in storage, but Captain Tucker said everything was destroyed. We'll need to find somewhere quick to live, I guess."

"Mister Jamie say we live here till we find house." There was a tone there that Dane decided to ignore. "Then we all live together. I like Mister Jamie. He good man. He very good to you."

"Yes, but that doesn't mean we'll stay together. I'm not exactly easy to...you know that people get scared around me. I don't want to get hurt again. Nathan...I don't know...I love James, Pi, but I don't know if he'll be able to stay with me."

"He good man. Love you. That's all that matter. Come, we go now. I wait all day and I want to find house."

Chapter 14

The apartment was trashed. Everything was destroyed just as they had been told. Food from the cabinets, cushions from the sofa, and chairs had been sliced open. Even the mattresses were cut up and tossed around the room. Jamie let Dane walk around and see it all. He'd asked his brother about it and Damon said that it would give her closure.

"There isn't anything here to save, is there? The only thing they didn't destroy is the answering machine. Oh, and there was that one towel that was still in the hamper. I don't even have any clothes to wear now. Pi and I will have to go to the storage place and pull out some of our clothes we had there. We hadn't planned to live here long anyway. Now this just makes it sooner, I guess." Dane had said this twice now. Jamie wanted to hold her, but didn't want her to be overwhelmed more.

"That's a good way to look at it. Maybe we could go shopping too. I'd love to help you find some sexy little undies and nighties to wear. Something I can tear from this very tasty body. Hummm, too bad Pi is just down the hall. I could press you against the wall and have my way with you, starting with that very wet pussy of yours."

She turned and looked at him. Jamie nearly did do what he had hoped would be a tease to make her smile.

"James. All you have to do is touch me and I feel like I'm going up in flames. I still want to taste your cock. I want to take you into my mouth and feel you come down my throat. I've never wanted to do that before, but with you, it's all I can think of."

"Christ, woman!" He adjusted his cock before he hurt himself. "I'm hard as rock and we are in no position to do anything about it. I want you. Do you think if we told Pi to stay away for...I don't know, an hour, she'd do it?"

"No. She has her mind set on finding a house. But think how much better it'll be when we do get alone. But tonight, I am going to have your cock in my mouth. Count on it."

Count on it? He could barely breathe. How the heck did she think he was going to count anything? Pulling her into his arms, he kissed her. Her mouth opened under his and his tongue tangled with hers. Reaching under her shirt, he slid his hand up and filled it with her warm breast. Her braless state made him moan and he tugged gently at her nipple.

"Lift your shirt for me. I need to taste you. And you have to be quiet this time. If you scream now, the entire neighborhood will come running."

Pulling her shirt up, she wrapped her fingers in his hair and held him to her breast as he tormented her nipple. Biting and nipping at her tender flesh had her rocking against his cock in the most erotic dance. Sliding his hand down her ass, he buried his two fingers against her heat and heard her hiss her approval.

"Dane, I need you. Now, I need to fuck you hard. I don't care who sees us or hears us. I need to be inside of you now."

Picking her up, he headed for the closet. It was the only place where the doors still shut. Taking her inside, he stood her on her feet and reached for her snap and zipper as she began pulling at his belt. When she had his pants undone, she reached inside and wrapped her hand around him. He nearly came right then.

"Turn around. This is going to be dirty, hard, and fast. I'm not going to last once you clamp over me."

Jerking her pants down to her ankles and not bothering to pull them off, he opened his pants and pushed her forward so that she was bent to her waist. He reached around her front, rubbed his fingers over her clit, and nearly sobbed with relief to find her wet and ready. Using his free hand, he guided his cock and slammed hard into her.

When Dane braced one hand against the wall and the other fisted in her mouth, he pulled nearly out to the tip and slammed home again. Over and over until he knew she was close. Leaning over her as he rocked into her, he bit her shoulder and pulled her clit. Her climax rocked over him, pulling him with her. Hearing her whimper and scream behind her hand gave him something more and he slammed hard into her again, feeling a second climax hit him hard. Never had that happened before. Over and over he pumped into her until the last tremor faded away. He leaned on her back and held her beneath him.

"You're going to kill me, I swear. As much as I'd like to apologize for the quickie fuck in a dirty, trashed closet, I think if we'd have been in a bed, I'd be dead right now."

Her giggle made him smile. He would have laughed, but he was sure he didn't have the energy. Pulling out of her heat, he pulled her to him and held her.

"We'd better get dressed," Jamie told her regretfully. "Pi will be wondering what we're up to for so long and I'd hate to have to explain how you raped me in the closet. She'll be upset with you for messing up her well laid plans."

"Me! I did no such thing. I was looking for clothes to wear and you—" Kissing her quiet seemed the best solution. It was that or take her again. His body was certainly willing even if his cock was not.

They were just coming out when Pi walked in the door. Her knowing smile had Jamie blush like a man…well, a man who just got his world rocked. Wrapping his arm around Dane, he winked at Pi.

"Well, ladies, how about if we go find us a house? I, for one, think we've done all we can here. Insurance will take care of the rest. Pi, where to next?"

~~~

Devin answered his phone, though he did not know the number. He was aware that as an attorney, his clients needed to get in touch with him, but it was Saturday and he was at home.

"Mr. Grant? It's Dane Wallace. I was wondering if you could help me out. I have this…I don't know my grandmother's attorney and I need to contact him. I know that it's your day off, but I would like to speak to him about something my grandmother left me."

"Of course, Dane. Please, call me Devin. Do you know his name? I have a list of numbers here and if I can't find it, then I can go to the office. Do you mind me asking what it is you're needing to speak to him about?"

"A house, her house, my grandmother's house. She left it to me in her will. I should have seen to it before now, but I…I didn't know what I wanted to do with it." He could hear her sigh before she continued. "Now with having no home, I think maybe Pi and I could stay there a few months until we decided. I wanted to get the key so we can look around. His name is Dexter, Martin Dexter. Do you know him?"

Devin almost asked where Jamie fit into this, but knew it was none of his business. Jamie was a big boy and if he and this woman were going to have a relationship, if they didn't already, then he would not get in the way.

"Yes, I know Martin. Let me see what I can do then I'll call you back. This number, is it yours? Can I call you back there?"

"Yes, or James' number. We're about to go into this other house now, but I think Pi has already crossed it off her list. She's said the sidewalks are too narrow. Why she cares, I don't...Mr. Grant, I was wondering...do you think maybe I could...I would like to set up a time and talk to you about something. Do you think I could see you? Professionally?"

"Of course, Dane. I'll call you back as soon as I talk to Martin. I'm sure you'll be coming to my mom's tomorrow. We'll talk then about setting up an appointment."

Devin hung up and picked up the house phone to call Martin. Devin liked Martin Dexter. He was an older attorney and he'd been in the private sector for a good many years. He answered on the second ring, laughing as he did.

"Devin, you young pup, have you done something to that lovely wife of yours and she wants to divorce you? I hope so. Give me a chance at that young thing."

"Stay away from my wife, you old womanizer, before I tell your wife," Devin said with a laugh. "If she knew half the things I know about you then she'd be the one divorcing you."

"Ha! Shows what you know. If she knew half the stuff you knew, she'd have hired a hit man and killed me. Divorce is much too painless for what she'd do to me. I know that you didn't call to see about my love life. What can I do for you? Good Christ, your mother isn't trying to bleed more money out of me, is she? She's a frightening woman when it comes to her charities."

"No. Not yet at any rate. I'm calling about Dane Wallace. She called me to see if she could look at her grandmother's house tonight. She said she doesn't know you and felt a little uncomfortable calling you cold like this."

Devin heard the chair squeak and some papers shuffle around. He could hear Martin talking to someone else then a door shut. Devin sat up in his chair as well. He knew this could not be good.

"How well do you know this girl?" Martin voice was different now, more professional. "The reason I ask is because the vultures have been waiting for her to land. She'll need someone to handle her. No, that's not what I mean. She'll need a good attorney to help her. Do you know much about this estate?"

"No. She's dating my brother Jamie." Devin took out a pad of paper and his pen. "It's becoming serious, I think. I know she just moved here from China since her grandmother passed away. And until tonight, I didn't know there was a house. Why?"

"The girl has money." Then Martin laughed. "She's a very, very wealthy woman. Scary wealthy. Her grandmother left her everything. The house? It's just the tip of the iceberg. I have the keys, I'll give them to you, but you should tell her that she needs to find her someone to go over everything with her. You should do it. She's going to need someone she can trust."

"I thought you were her attorney." Devin would never step on anyone's toes. "I mean, why aren't you 'seeing to her?' You've been the family attorney for a while now, haven't you?"

"I retired as of six months ago. When her grandmother passed, I decided I'd had enough. She was a wonderful old bird, but I made more than enough money off her to live several lifetimes. No, Ms. Wallace needs someone young and savvy. Someone who doesn't need her money and doesn't mind telling her what she needs to do."

"You've not met her then, have you? Dane is the type of woman who has no problem telling you to get fucked and offering to hire someone to do it to you. I saw her punch Jamie in the nose for thinking he could tell her what to do." Devin smiled at the unabashed laughter that came back through the line at him.

"More like her granny than I thought then. Her mother was a bitch. Worst kind of bitch. Mrs. Messenger told her mother that she had to leave her monies to her when she got sick, but she had better never leave anything to Dane. Mrs. Sharp just nodded and as soon as the old buzzard was dead, she changed her will to leave everything to her granddaughter. Best damned day of my life. We laughed about it for weeks on end."

"Just how much are we talking here? I know the Messenger estate was big, but I haven't a clue what Mrs. Sharp was about."

"Well, with monies, insurance, and holding, including the houses and all the corporations, Danish Messenger Wallace is worth just under eight billion dollars, making her one of the riches women in the world. Of course, that doesn't include the personal checking account that was set up for Danish when her mother died, nor the jewelry that is still locked in the safes — one here and two in the house on Rector Street."

"Holy Fucking Christ," Devin shouted. Eight billion plus. And she was living in that crappy townhouse without a good lock and second hand furniture.

"Yeah, that's what I thought too. Makes you sit up and take notice, don't it? There is no one to contest the will. Danish was an only child, as was her mother. Her father is deceased, died some years ago after Danish was born. The only living person left is her. Like I said, she's going to need someone to help her out. Up for the job?"

After a few more minutes of talking, Martin told Devin he'd send over all the important information to him on Monday morning. He was no longer her attorney and thought that if Devin did not do it, then he could guide Danish to someone who could and would do a good job for her.

Devin sat in his chair for several minutes trying to wrap him mind around that much money. Glancing at his watch, he got up to find Veronica. He had to meet Martin in twenty minutes at a coffee shop on Tenth.

"You should come with me," he told his wife. "Maybe you could help Dane with her house hunting. She could probably use a friend about now. Plus, if she becomes a part of this family, we'll need to know her better."

"Hummm...okay, what do you know that you're not telling me, and why?" He glanced at her and tried to look innocent. "I already like her. And I doubt she needs my help finding a house. Give it up, Devin, what's going on?"

"What do you mean? I just want to get to...well, shit, Veronica, can't I get anything past you? I want you to see how close she is to Jamie. I just found out that she's not as broke as I first assumed. She's quiet wealthy as a matter of fact and with that sort of money comes all sorts of people out of the woodwork. I don't want Jamie to be hurt because someone else comes along with a better line."

"You arrogant ass. I should smack you, do you know that? First of all, Jamie is nearly thirty years old and secondly, if you so much as hint to him that you know this, I'll make you sleep in the guest bedroom for the next fifty years. And I'll wear nothing to bed every night to taunt you. Any idiot can see that they love each other and a few bucks isn't going to make much difference." She stood now. "I'm going with you. You need a keeper. And just so you know, I'm telling your mom."

She fussed at him all the way to the coffee shop and then sat in stunned silence on the way to the house to meet Dane, Jamie, and Pi. Veronica started to go over the papers Martin gave them when they left. Since looking at the total worth, Veronica had not said a word.

"I told you she was wealthy. I don't know what you're surprised about." Her glare made him burst out laughing. To be honest, it was nice to know that he hadn't heard the older man wrong. Christ, love a duck, eight billion dollars!

"What do you plan to tell her, Devin? I doubt that she has any idea about all this." Devin thought she might be right. "I think if it were me, I'd have to find a place to hide until I got a better handle on it."

"Nothing. I'm not her attorney and until she hears from Martin severing his business with the estate, there isn't anything I can do. I'll agree with him, she does need someone to guide her through this, but if she and Jamie marry, I'm not so sure I should have anything to do with her money."

"You think she'd think you were cheating her? I doubt that she'd believe that. She is the most upstanding person I know. And you are the most honest I know." She looked at him as he continued. "She couldn't do better in an attorney than you."

"Thank you, love, but I was thinking of mixing family with business. It's okay with the little stuff I do now, helping with Spencer's divorce, guiding Byr thought the right channels to set up his business, and Damon's malpractice insurance, but billions of dollars is beyond even my scope. No, I think she needs someone to help her and it shouldn't be me."

"So if she asks, you'll turn her down?" Veronica asked sadly.

"Hell no! If she asks, I'm going to try and triple her money in five years. I'm not stupid."

Chapter 15

Dane gave the address to Jamie and he drove them to the house. He said he was not familiar with the area so he had to plug the information into the GPS to get them there. Dane was nervous. She did not know what to expect and then Devin had said he needed to speak to her as soon as possible.

"Shit, Dane, is this it? I thought you said it was a house. This is a friggin' mansion." And it was.

"I was only here once as a child. My mother hated to come here and I was never allowed to visit her after I turned eight. Every time I came home after I left to live in China, Grandmother and I would meet in New York. I'd forgotten it was so big. Too big probably for just us."

She didn't know whether to include James in her "us" status. He said they'd all live together, but that was when they were living at his house. Before she could say anything more, another car pulled up.

"Wow! You lived here? Dane, this is beautiful! How many bedrooms does it have, thirty?" Ronnie said with a laugh. Dane was glad she had come with Devin. He made her nervous. Well, all the Grant men did.

"Actually, you're not far off. Including the pool house, there are twenty bedrooms and twenty-five baths. Each bedroom has a private bath. In addition to the formal and informal dining rooms, there are several other rooms — let's see, library, study, office, conference room, something called a cloth room, and a nursery. Martin gave me this to give to you." Devin handed her a folder. "I think there's an indoor and outdoor pool too. My grandmother loved to swim. I do as well. I don't think we can live here. It's too big."

"Missy Dane, you live here with me and Mister Jamie. He look like he want to fill house with babies. It be good for you. I be granny to them. Let's go in. I want to see kitchen."

Dane heated with embarrassment. It did not get any better when Devin threw back his head and laughed too. She couldn't even glance at James. What on earth was the matter with Pi? Taking the key from Devin, they went up the front steps.

"Martin said there was a staff house just off to the left. When Mrs. Sharp went into the hospital the last time, she had the house closed up. The staff was elderly anyway and was ready for retirement. He said that if you needed it, he had a list of people who want to come and apply to work for you." Devin handed her this list as well.

The entrance hall was magnificent. The huge oak double doors opened silently to a massive stairwell that stretched back and separated to go right and left at the top. The crystal chandelier was covered on the top with a heavy drape. Dane supposed it was to keep the dust off. The floor was white and black tile and there were several vases that graced the walls of deep ruby red.

"The only time I was here, Mr. Carter, the butler, showed me how to slide down the banister without falling off the end and hurting myself. We spent the entire day practicing. When Grandmother came home from her meeting, I was just sliding down and fell off the end when I saw her. She handed her coat to Mr. Carter and walked toward me. I remember thinking that I was going to get beaten. She simply walked to the top, threw her leg over, and rode down like a pro. She told me that she'd had more fun doing that than anything. We spent the whole next day together doing things that I wished I could have done with my mother." Dane looked up the staircase and said, "Actually, that's not true. I'm glad I have those memories with just her. She was a wonderful woman."

"Dane, I have to ask you something," Ronnie asked her quietly when they were walking around. "I know that you have every right to be pissed about it, but honey, is your first name really Danish? When Martin called you that when I called him, I never thought about it. Then I saw it on some of the papers. Seriously, your mother called you Danish?"

"No, that's my middle name. My first name is something worse, far worse. She never wanted me, you see. My father left her after she told him that she was much too far along to have me aborted. He begged her to let him raise me, but she said that it was her duty to do so. That's why she wouldn't let my grandmother raise me. So I grew up in Chicago where I could get to the best schools, she said. I think it was because she could hide among the thousands of others in the city, yet not be overlooked with her money. My mother thought being rich was the only way people should be."

"What a horrible bitch. I'm sorry, sweetie, but she was. I don't know how you turned out to be so sweet and have her as a mother," Ronnie said.

"I never spoke to my mother for ten years while I lived at home and after the thing with the murders, I never saw her again. If not for the household staff that lived there, I probably would have been dead by now. They cared for me when she wouldn't and fed me when I was being punished. I owe them a great deal. And then when I ran away to China, I had Pi. Well, we had each other. She is my best friend and the closest thing to a mother I've ever had. But enough sad stuff, let's have a look at this monstrosity."

Ronnie, Pi, and Dane went to the left, the men up the stairs. One of the dining rooms was set up with a long table with twenty chairs down each side and one at each end. There were several pieces of pottery that sat in three different places on the table and a large chandelier in the middle with two smaller ones to each side. The floor was a deep wood and the fireplace took up one entire wall. The one across from it was a china cabinet filled with stacks of dinnerware and glasses with what looked like a crest on it. Dane stepped closer and recognized the emblem that had been on the front door. The credenza beneath it was filled with linens and silverware. Dane wondered about the security and made a mental note to ask someone. There was a door leading out and they went through it into a smaller yet no less elegant dining room. This table was a duplicate of the one in the larger room only there were eight chairs along the sides and one at each end. The chandelier was a single hanging light. This one, too, was covered. The dishes here were white without any other design. The floor was also wood, but there was a large area run of oriental design that covered most of the floor. Moving through this room, they walked into the kitchen.

The kitchen was made to accommodate the dining rooms and all the guests it would hold. There was an eight burner gas stove, a walk in refrigerator, and also a walk in freezer. The cook island was long and the stainless steel gleamed in the overhead light. The floors, a bright white with grout a dark blue, had an occasional blue tile around the room. The tile that went around the room along the walls was the same colors of deep indigo blue and white. Pots and pans hung from the ceiling with stacks of them under the worktable. Three dishwashers and two sinks took up one wall and a large window topped the counters above them. Every appliance known to man and some that maybe did not, graced the shelves along another wall. Pi was in heaven. She could not seem to stop touching everything and pointing out something new every time she circled the room.

"Oh, Missy Dane, this my kitchen. We set up house here and I be happy Chinese woman forever. I never ask for another thing. You have hot food and I even make you American food when you want. I can cook anything here."

"What if the rest of the house is crap? Then what will we do? Let you come by here and cook every day?" Dane said, laughing.

"I think you could probably live in this kitchen. Damn, but this is one huge house. I volunteer you to have the next holidays here. We could come and live here and you'd never know it." Ronnie opened a door and nodded to Pi. "Hey, check it out. I found you a room to live in."

The walk in pantry rivaled most grocery stores. It was a big as the entire townhouse that she and Pi had lived in until recently, and Pi's entire house in China. It was forty feet long and twenty feet wide. There were shelves along every wall and a double one down the middle. The shelves where empty, but Dane had no doubt that when her grandmother was living, they were packed tight with staples and anything else that might be needed to feed an army. By the time they were coming back through the dining rooms, Jamie and Devin were coming down the stairs.

"There are twelve bedrooms down each hall, six on each side. Each room is as big as a small apartment. There's even a fireplace in each room and a settee area. The beds are all stripped and the furniture is covered. The bathrooms have both a shower and a tub and a linen closet just inside the bath. We're guessing the master suite is down here somewhere. Want to help us find it?" Jamie wiggled his brows at her and she laughed.

Before they found the master suite, they found two living rooms, a library, and a study. There was a very masculine office next to the study that smelled of cigar smoke and cologne. And they found what could only be the cloth room.

The room's walls where covered in tapestry. Old and new, there must have been over a hundred of them. Some were behind glass. Others hung on antique hangers and had faded over time. There was a round chair that sat in the middle of the room that was white, as was the carpet on the floor. What little walls showed had pin striped silver and white wall paper. Dane remembered this room.

"Grandmother would come in here a couple of times a day. She said it was her paradisiacal room. She told me that when I got older, I'd need a room like this. She said I would need somewhere I could go and let the day's events wash away. She told me my grandfather collected these for her. And that she could never part with them because of it."

Dane picked up one of the smaller pieces and held it to her cheek. It was softer than she thought it would be and she felt tears fill her eyes. Before she could turn away, Jamie walked up behind her and pulled her back against his chest. Closing her eyes, she leaned into him.

"Dane, do you think we could live here? It's up to you, but I think you look happy here. There are so many memories that you have. I know it's big—hell, it's fucking huge, but we can hire people to help run it."

"James, I love you very much, but you know this can't last. I'm a freak and I don't want to hurt you. I know I will, but—"

"Dane, I love you too. And I'm going to tell you that every day for the rest of our lives. We'll hurt each other, I'm not so naive to think what we have is perfect, but I'm willing to give it my best shot. And if I hear you call yourself a freak again, I'm going to put soap on your tongue."

They both laughed and he turned her in his arms. The kiss was gentle, a whisper of a touch as he brushed over her lips. Then after another touch, he deepened the kiss and touched his tongue to hers. Hunger consumed her; need to touch and to be touched surged over her. Groaning deep in her chest, she wrapped her arms around his neck and pressed her body to his. When he reached down and lifted her by her ass, she wrapped her legs around his hips and tightened around him. His answering growl moved along her veins like heated molten lava.

"Christ, I can't get enough of you. I find myself looking for places to ram you up against and fuck every second I'm around you. I'm getting to the point where I almost don't care who's around when I do it either. Let's find the master bedroom and break it in right now."

"Uhhh, Jamie, you might want to wait on that," Devin said from behind them. "There is a security officer here to see the owner of the house. Seems that Martin didn't tell me there was an alarm system. He's right now calling in back up. Pi is going at him with a broom."

Dane took off running and only got lost once. By the time she skidded to a stop in the front hall, Pi was on the floor in cuffs and Ronnie was screaming that she was going to have his badge by the end of the day. It might have been funny if

Dane had not been so embarrassed — both by the guard and Devin overhearing her and James.

"This is my house. If you could let my...my mother go then I'll show you some identification. These are my attorneys, Devin and Veronica Grant. My grandmother Savannah Sharp left this to me and this is the first time I've been out to see it."

"The alarm went off and we had no prior knowledge of anyone being here, Miss...Messenger. I'm sure you understand that we—"

"Actually, I don't. Understand I mean." Dane's voice was sharp and hard. "We've been here for a good hour and you're just now showing up? That doesn't bode well for the security of this home, do you think? I mean, what if I had been living here already? Could I expect the same sort of service from your firm? Mr. Grant, if you could make note for us to find another firm as soon as possible then—"

"Now see here. This is our beat and we take care of—" The officer sputtered.

"When I speak, you will not interrupt me. I pay the bills, not you. As soon as I start to work for you, then you can say all you want and I'll listen. Now, I want you off my property right now. And if I don't have a formal written apology from you and your firm by end of business day Monday on the way you've treated my mother and my home, I will sue your ass. Then not only will you be out of a job, but every member of your 'back-up' will as well. Have I made myself perfectly clear?"

She didn't think he was going to answer. She was also afraid that he might. Just when she was going to back off, he did.

"Yes, ma'am, I understand. I'll let my superiors know that you have made demands...requests to that effect immediately. But in my defense, I was —"

"You'd do well to leave well enough alone. I'm in no mood to fuck with you anymore today. Leave or I'll send my hounds after you. And by hounds, I mean the best attorneys in the state."

He left without another word and when he pulled out of the drive, Dane was surprised that he did not spin his tires, but he drove out sedately and within the speed limits. Grabbing the back of the chair next to her, she dropped into in and put her head between her knees.

"Wow, remind me never to piss you off. I think you left claw marks he'll feel for a very long time. I think you'd better find yourself a new security firm quick. I doubt they'll be making a quick trip out here for anything. Unless it's to watch the house burn down," Ronnie said as she sat on the floor in front of her. "You all right, honey?"

"No. Yes. I think so. Maybe. I can depend on you two, right? I mean as my attorneys? I know that the estate is big, I'm not sure how big, but I'll need someone I can depend on. Will you do it for me?"

"Dane, honey, we should talk before you decide that. This estate isn't big, it's massive," Devin said above her. "I've never handled anything this big before. You might be better off going to a bigger firm for them to keep it straight for you."

"How much is it, Devin? Mr. Dexter told you, didn't he? Tell me." He looked uncomfortable. Dane was afraid it was bad, very bad.

"Honey, you should really do this in —"

"Tell me, damn it!" she snapped. "I'm tired of people treating me like some sort of idiot. How much is it worth?"

"Eight billion. Everything? Its seven point seven four billion dollars. You're not rich, Dane, you're scary rich. That's what Martin said anyway." Devin smiled. "I think he might be right."

"Holly carp, Missy Dane! We buy two houses."

Chapter 16

Jamie looked over at Dane and waited for her to say something. Anything. He was not sure what he could say; the numbers kept circling around in his head like a merry-go-round. Even as a math professor, he was having a difficult time visualizing eight billion dollars. When she stood up and sat down again for the second time, he turned to the wall of glasses and opened the cabinets beneath it. Perfect.

Pouring her a half a tumbler of the dark liquid, he handed it to her. "Here, baby, drink this." He should have said sip, but by the time he'd realized that, Dane had tossed the bourbon back like a pro. Coughing hard did not stop her from glaring at him.

"I need to take a walk. No, I need to…can I borrow your car?" She looked at him. "I need to get away for just a few…for just a little while. I won't be gone long."

Jamie wanted to go with her, but knew that she needed to work this out on her own. Reaching into his pants, he handed her the keys. When she leaned in and kissed him, he wanted to shout to the world, but simply kissed her again.

"Missy Dane, we sleep here tonight? I find sheets. We make big party. I order pizza from Daddy place. Okay?" Pi said, just a little nervous.

"Yes, I'll pick it up on my way...I just realized I don't have any money. I have more money than I'll ever spend in my lifetime and I don't have a single penny on me." Her laughter scared Jamie a little and when he started to reach for her, Ronnie pulled out her purse.

"Come on, Dane. you and I will go visit a friend. Devin, you and Jamie fix up a few bedrooms. I'll call the nanny and have her bring Marie here. Pi, why don't you see what you need in the kitchen in the way of groceries? Then tomorrow we'll go shopping for whatever you need."

When Ronnie leaned in and kissed him, she whispered in his ear that she would take good care of her. With a quick kiss on the cheeks, both women were gone. Jamie looked over at his brother who looked pole axed.

"So, do you think she's good for the money?" Devin looked at him for several seconds then threw back his head and laughed. The tension was broken but not the bomb.

"I have a client worth more than all of our combined assets. Christ, wait until I tell Nicky. He'll shit a brick. I'll have to hire an accountant and someone just to watch over her money. Holy shit, eight billion."

"Yeah, that's a lot." He started up the stairs, not caring if he followed or not. She was worth more than anyone he knew. And this house...how the hell could he expect her to stay with him, a lowly teacher, when she had all this.

"Jamie?" Devin yelled as Jamie cleared the stairs. "What's up? You don't think she's going to change, do you? My God, that woman loves you. Why I have no idea, but there you have it. This isn't going to change her. You have to believe that."

"Yeah, sure. Let's get her house put together. I never did find the master bedroom. Do you think she'll want to—"

"Jamie, look at me." Devin turned him around. "She loves you. This won't change anything. It's not going to change the woman that she is."

"Sure it will, Devin. Like she said, she has more money than she can spend in several lifetimes. I'll fix up the bedroom down here. I just need a few minutes. I'll be all right."

He hurt. His heart felt…trampled. He did not know if it was because she wanted to be alone and had taken Ronnie, or that she did not want him with her. He walked into the biggest bedroom he'd ever seen and sat on the unmade bed. Even this room screamed money. Laying back, he closed his eyes.

~~~

They'd been driving for about ten minutes when Dane realized she was with Ronnie. She looked over at the other woman and frowned. How the hell did that happen? She supposed that it was a good thing she was not driving.

"Where are we going? I don't remember leaving the house. Pizza, I remember pizza. Why are you driving?" Dane looked around. She had no clue where they were.

"I have money, you don't. I was wondering if you've talked to Cait. She feels really bad about what happened to you that day. I know that you and her have a history, but I think you two need to clear the air. Especially now."

"Why especially now?" Dane looked out the windows. "You know I've never met a nosier bunch of people in my life as you guys. Are there any boundaries you guys don't cross? All I wanted to do was keep a man from getting killed and my past has come up and snapped my butt, I've had my apartment trashed, and now I'm going to visit someone who hates me. I'm not saying you guys are to blame for all that, but still."

Truth be told, she really couldn't blame them for any of it, but she was rambling. A person did not have to make sense when they rambled. If there wasn't a rule about that, there should be.

"Especially now that you and Jamie are getting married," Ronnie went on. "You are going to marry him, aren't you? They can be pushy at times, the Grant men, but they love you more than you'll ever be loved or ever hope to be loved." Dane wondered who left this woman in charge and realized that no one would have left her in charge. She'd have knocked the crap out of the person in the front of the line and taken over. Probably killed the other leader with one fist tied behind her back.

"Hold on a second there! Married? I don't think so. Married? Why would he want to marry me? As my mother used to say...fuck her. She didn't love me, why should I quote her? I don't think James had any plans in making our...relationship? Whatever it is, I don't think he plans to make it permanent. We're having a great time in bed. Yeah, we love each other, but that doesn't mean...why would he want to marry me?" Dane felt her heart pound in her chest. Marry?

"You know you keep asking me that," Ronnie said with a laugh. "Maybe you should ask him. And loving someone is a great reason to marry someone. Is it the money? I would imagine that would make a difference in someone's life, but Jamie has had money all his life. And you too for that matter. What's a few billion between lovers?"

"The money? No, I don't care about the money. It just makes it so we can do what we want when we...you know, you're scary. I am not marrying James. Besides, it's a moot point. He's never asked. I would think that's a pretty important thing when two people make the decision to get

married, don't you? One of them should ask the other? What
are you doing now?"

They had pulled up in front of the hospital. Dane had a
scary thought that Ronnie was going to knock her block off
and then throw her out of the door as she zoomed past. She
really needed to take a break here. These sort of thoughts
were nuts.

"Get out. Cait's room is two thirty-four. She might have
little Paddy in there so try not to piss her off too much. It
might sour her milk. Go up there and play nice. I'll be back in
an hour. Don't worry. I'll make sure the guys know where we
are."

Not really knowing why, Dane slipped out of the car and
shut the door. Before she could turn back and ask again what
she was doing there, Ronnie took off like the hounds of hell
were after her. Yes, I really need a break.

Dane wandered around the hospital for several minutes.
Then found the gift shop. She didn't have any money, but she
did have a credit card. She had to stop the slightly crazed
giggle that burst forth as she thought about if she could make
the payment next month.

She knew as soon as she saw it that it was perfect. Picking
it up carefully, she took the little gift to the cashier and set it
down. She asked if she could leave it there. She needed to get
a couple more things, and went back to shopping. A hundred
and twenty-three dollars later, she was headed to room two
thirty-four.

Once she got off the elevator, she wasn't sure what to do.
Did she just knock and go in? What if she was nursing her kid
or something? What if the family was in there? She paced for
several minutes with her hands full of little bags until one of
the nurses started staring at her. Taking a deep breath, she
knocked and when granted, she walked in.

She didn't know what she expected, but seeing Cait in a rocking chair crying was not one of them. Dane had never been good around tears with adults and now was no different. Setting the bags on the bed, she sat in the chair across from her.

"Did pushy butt tell you I was coming and you're unhappy because your gun is in your other pants? I think we should use it on her. She made me come up here."

"Are you wishing you hadn't? I'm glad you're here. And 'pushy butt?' That could be anyone of the Grant woman – including you. And have you met Margaret? Christ, that woman will steam roll you in a second if you let her. No, post baby blues, I guess. I was feeling sorry for myself."

She decided to ignore the comment about her being a Grant woman. She was frankly getting a little upset about the conversation. Dane walked over and looked down at the infant asleep in the little crib. She'd never held one so small and wanted to hold this one. She looked back at Cait.

"May I hold him? Oh, I have something for him and the little girl, I don't know her name. You too."

"Dane, I wanted to tell you how—"

"Please don't. Let's move on from here, all right? That is if you can forgive me. I've done some...some incredibly stupid things in my life and though I've tried hard not to hurt people, I know I have. Especially then. My mother was...she wasn't a nice person. And for reasons I can only guess, she hated me. I tried, every day I tried to do things she wanted me to, to be the girl she needed me to be. But those children..." Dane ran her finger down Paddy's cheek. "I could save them, Cait, and I did. But it cost me so much. I think it cost us both so much. Can you forgive me?"

Instead of answering, Cait got up and went to the crib. She picked up her son and handed him to Dane. Then hugged her. Dane held her close too. She had never felt such wonderful emotions from someone, and returned them.

"Shit! I felt that! You can do that? That must be really weird when you and Jamie have sex!"

Dane could only stare at her open mouthed. She felt heat stain her cheeks as she turned away. These people were beyond anything she'd ever encountered.

"I'm not sure about that. He seems okay with it. He doesn't really…complain, I guess." She sat on the chair again, holding the baby. "I keep waiting for him to freak out. To run screaming into the night."

"Dane, you can talk to—"

"You know, I should have asked your sizes when I left," Ronnie said as she entered the room, her hands full of bags. "I had a hell of a time getting something…what's happened? Damn it, I thought you two would kiss and make up. Now everyone is going to be pissed at me. I'm sorry, guys. I thought that getting you together would help you both."

"Nothing happened," Dane said without moving. "And what do you need my sizes for? Ohmigod! You bought me a straight jacket, didn't you?"

"No, I bought you a negligee. It's black. I have one sort of like it. Well, now I have one just like it. I thought you could use it with your new house. Jamie will love it."

"You want me to parade around in my new house in a black negligee? I don't think so. I mean, you're nice and…well, you're pushy, but I suppose you mean well. But I draw the line at having matching underwear. You'll have to take it back." Dane laughed at her expression, but continued.

"You bought a new house? Cool, what's it look like? Can I come see it as soon as they release me? I love our house. Is it big?"

"It's huge!" Ronnie squealed. "Twenty-five bedrooms and two flipping dining rooms. You should see this thing. And it's furnished too! Devin and I are staying tonight, if the guys can find sheets. Which reminds me, Devin called. He thinks you should knock some sense into Jamie. I don't know what happened, but he said he hasn't come out of the bedroom since we left."

Dane felt as if her heart had stopped beating. He figured out something. She was not really sure what, but knew that he had made a decision and that she was not going to like it. Feeling tears fill her eyes, she looked down at the baby.

"I'd like to go now please. I have to...could we please go now? Thank you, Cait. I'll...he probably...I'm really sorry, could we go?"

Neither woman said anything to her as she handed the baby back to Cait. Or if they did, she did not hear them. Moving as though in a bad dream, she and Ronnie left the hospital and went to the car. Dane vaguely remembered stopping once, and the smell of pizza making her slightly sick, but nothing else. When she got to the house, she was out of the car before it stopped completely. She went to the bedroom with the pink shopping bag still in her hand.

Chapter 17

Jamie heard the door open and close, but did not open his eyes. It wasn't until the bed dipped that he thought it might not be Devin. He looked over at Dane who sat on the edge of the bed with a bright pink bag on her lap as she cried.

"Dane? What is it? Are you—"

"I'm really sorry. I told you that I'd hurt…do you know that my ex-husband took an ad out in the paper telling people what a freak I am? Of course most people didn't understand it. He wasn't smart enough to put the stupid thing in Chinese. And the few people who could read it didn't care. Then there was the fact that I couldn't have children. I forgot to tell you that. I'm sorry about that too. His mother had me tested after we were married. I didn't tell her I was on the pill so I couldn't get pregnant, but when the ad came out and I found out, I just stopped taking it. What was the point? Anyway, I'm sorry. You should probably go, huh?"

Jamie didn't say anything. He didn't know what had happened between the time that she left and now, but he was reasonably sure that something had. He reached over and took the bag from her, intending to hold her and figure it out when it spilled on the floor.

He picked it up and looked at what it was. "Christ, Dane! Is this for me? Oh, honey, I love it."

"You'll look silly in it. Your sister-in-law bought it for me, or you, I guess. But she bought it before she talked to Devin. You know they're a pushy, nosey bunch of people." She tried to snatch it back from him.

Devin? He tried to think what happened to have Devin upset Dane and remembered snippets of what he'd said to his brother. Shit! He'd fucked it up royally—him and Devin.

"Dane, will you put this on for me? I'd really like to see it on you before you make me go home. And yes, they are pushy and nosey, but I think they mean well. Go put it on for me. Please?"

He put the tiny pieces of sheer lace in her hand and pushed her up off the bed. When he guided her to the bathroom and she went inside, he did a little jig. Then he looked around the room. He stripped off the bed and found the linens someone had put on the trunk at the bottom of the bed. Rushing around, he put the sheets on then threw the comforter over them. Going to the fireplace, he was pleased to see that it was electric, and turned on the flames. He was just standing up again when the door opened. Mother fuck!

Dane had let her hair down and it fell in soft waves down her back. The nightie or whatever it was called was...magnificent. The top was a barely there see thru bit of lace that hugged her breasts like a second skin. The tiny ribbons that tied at her shoulders strained to hold her. The lace that covered her full breasts did not hide her nipples, which were erect and hard. The front of it tied together with another little ribbon and hung open to the bottom. A triangle of lace and more ribbon covered her mound and nothing else. His mouth both watered at the sight before him and dried at the same time. He could not move, words failed him, and his body was on fire.

"I've never worn anything like this before. I don't think it covers much, does it? Do you like it?"

Her voice sounded unsure and if he had not been so totally focused on her, he might have missed it. He looked at her face and could see that she didn't have a clue how beautiful she was. He started toward her slowly and spoke softly.

"I'm going to buy you one of these every night for the rest of our lives. I want to take it from your body slowly and rip it from you at the same time. I want to peel away each inch of it to taste your skin and I want to ravage you quickly. I have never in all my life seen a more luscious, beautiful creature in my life. Dane, I love you so much, I ache with it. I ache with a need to show you, to prove to you that I love you beyond everything else."

"You're not leaving me?" Dane asked. "When Ronnie said that you were locked in here after we left, I thought you might have changed your mind. I know that I'm not exactly what a man wants in a partner, but I thought we could have more fun while we're together. I have to tell you something. It's important, all right?"

He looked at her and was a little nervous. Nodding, he stepped back a step and waited. She would not look at him and he wanted to tilt her face up so that he could see, but wanted her to take her own time.

"I can't have children. I'm sorry, I should have told you sooner, but I never…he didn't tell me until we were married and I…Nathan took out this whole page ad telling everyone that he was divorcing me and why. Among my freakish abilities, he also said I was barren. Actually, people were more upset about that than my ability to read their emotions.

But I can't have your child. I'm so sorry, James." She flushed. "I know that's a bit…you know, premature, but I thought you should know."

He was hurt at first, no children, but then he thought about her and having her. She was his. He was going to find this ex-husband of hers someday and beat the ever-loving shit out of him if it was the last thing he ever did.

~~~

"Baby, we'll just have to figure out another way to have children. There are lots of children out there that we could adopt. I don't care about that. Well, I do, but not as much as I love you. Dane, I know this is probably the worst timing, but will you marry me? Will you please become my wife? I don't have a ring, but I do love you."

She walked to him, wrapped her arms around his neck, and pulled him in to her mouth. She was not shy this time, but opened her mouth over his and took. Sliding his hands into the opening of her top, he pulled her to him.

Using restraint he did not know he had, he kissed her back, gentling the kiss and pulling back from her slightly. Time, he was going to take his time with her. He was going to make love to her.

Reaching up, he untied one ribbon at her shoulder and watched as it dropped down. The material was so tight over her breast it did not fall but clung to her. He took the ribbon and pulled it down slowly until her nipple caught on the lace. Using his tongue, he wet the material and it let go, Dane moaned above him.

"I talked to Byron the other night about you. About how to make it so that you don't hold back on us. I want you to trust me tonight and do what I want, all right?"

"James, I'm not sure if I'd like to get into the games he plays, some but not all of them. He and Taylor are…more sexually advanced than I am." He should have known she'd know they were into bondage. Smiling at her, he untied the other ribbon.

"He said that I should tie you to the bed and have my way with you. That I should have you not come until you were nearly ready to explode or kill me one. Would you let me tie you up, Dane?"

"I'm ready to explode now. Please, you're going too slow. I want to feel you touch me. I want you inside of me."

He leaned down and took her nipple into his mouth and nipped at it. She surged against him with a hiss. Untying the last piece of ribbon between her breasts, he let the top fall to the floor. She was panting. Her hot breath sent heat coursing through his veins.

"I want you hotter. Lie down on the bed, put your arms above your head, and hold onto the headboard. Don't let go, not until I tell you to. Next time we go out, we're going to go shopping and buy us some toys to play with. I think we might enjoy them."

He watched as she moved to the bed. When she turned, he noticed the scars again and wanted to run his tongue over them and soothe her. But he knew if he touched her right now, he'd be inside of her in seconds. Watching her do as he asked, his cock ached to be free. He took off his shirt and pants but left his boxers on. No since in inviting more trouble.

Her breasts looked inviting with the flicker of flame reflecting off them. He dropped his knees on the floor beside her and rubbed the palm of his hand over the taut peak. Her arms strained to move, but she left them where he had told her to put them.

"I'm going to lick your entire body, Dane. Then when I'm finished, I'm going to start again. The thought of touching you and tasting you makes me ache in ways I've never felt before."

Removing his hand, he laved his tongue over the darkened areola and teased her nipple. When she moaned, he licked the underside of her breast and suckled at it, feeling the heavy flesh tighten more. Moving his mouth down her ribs, he licked and kissed each rib as he went. When he got to her hip, he bit her gently and watched as her hips rose up off the bed and undulated. He could smell her now, her arousal, her heat, and wanted to again rip the barrier away and feast on her tender folds.

Standing, he moved onto the bed, pulling her legs apart as he went. He sat on his knees between them and tried to decide where to go next. Her face captured him, her eyes dark as night, lips swollen from her biting them. A blush fanned over her cheeks as she looked back at him. Crawling up her body without touching her, he took her mouth. The kiss was hungry and sharp; their tongues dueled and danced. He tasted her need in the dark warmth and returned it to her. Pulling away and sitting back down was the hardest thing he'd ever done.

Starting at her ankles, he ran both hands up her calves and back down again. Over and over he skimmed her legs, his touch barely a whisper. Needing to see his effect on her, he untied the ribbons at her hips one at a time with his mouth pulling the tie slowly. When both sides were undone, he nipped it between his lips and pulled it away from her.

"Christ, James, you're killing me. Please, let me touch you. I need you to touch me, please?"

"No. Don't move or I'll stop. I'm enjoying this too much to hurry through it." He had no idea how he would have stopped, but the threat worked apparently because she didn't let go of the head board.

Her pussy was soaked. The soft curls were glistening with her juices and he wanted to bury his mouth over her and drink. Knowing that he would not be able to stop, he did run his long finger along the seam and then push inside of her.

Wet heat and a tight grip made him moan. Moving slowly in and out of her, he watched as she rode his finger. When he inserted a second then a third, he nearly came when she started begging him to fuck her.

"You want to come, baby, I need something from you. You have to let go and enjoy this. I want to feel what you're feeling not only when you come, but all the time we're in bed together."

"It's too much. You don't know what you're asking me. Please, let me come, you come inside of me."

Without answering her, he pulled out of her and licked his fingers. His cock wept for her. It was getting harder and harder, literally, to not give her what she wanted. He resumed his assault and leaned down and braced himself over her body.

With his mouth, he touched her, kissing and biting at her. For every bite he inflicted on her, he would kiss her. Nothing was left untouched, the indentation of her belly button, and the middle of her ribs, the small scar he found on her side, and the tiny mole he discovered on her pelvis. Each and every inch of her felt his tongue and mouth until he got to her breast.

He was trembling with need, his cock burning to be released. Looking into her eyes, he knew she was close and wanted to fall into her body, but he needed her to trust him, to trust them. Licking at her nipple, he blew across it then gently dropped by degrees onto her body. His legs and hips settled between hers, his torso scraped over her nipples, and he felt his tighten with hers. His mouth covered hers, taking and giving all that he could.

He felt her stiffen, her body tightening under him. Then he felt her moving into him, her mind merging with his. He was flooded with sensations, images of what she wanted, what she needed. He was not sure how to give back, but he thought about what he was feeling, how she felt beneath him, how she tasted when he kissed her, nipped at her. His body shuddered with need, rippled with pleasure. Moving up again, he took off his briefs, getting tangled in them, and finally settled once again between her legs.

Fisting his cock, he nudged at her entrance and felt the heat, her wet answering need to his pull at him. Slowly, almost reverently, he entered her. Pushing to seat himself inside of her, he felt her tighten around him, and nearly came from that alone. Pulling out slowly, he moved back in, feeling everything she felt, his cock as it brushed against her, stretching her open to take him. Moving faster, rocking into her harder, he cupped her breast, took it into his mouth, and suckled her, first one then the other, while rolling the other nipple between his fingers. When he felt her come, her body convulsing under him, he lifted his chest off hers and pumped into her. Hard and quick, his climax grabbed him tight and he roared into her, filling her and emptying himself of his seed. He kept moving into her, feeling her come again and again until the last tremor left her. He fell over her, sinking them both into the bed. Rolling to his back, he took her over with him and settled them both comfortably. His heated skin did not need a blanket, but he knew that later they would. He reached to the bottom of the bed, pulled the light blanket over them, and slipped into a deep sleep.

~~~

Dane woke the next afternoon to an empty house. Jamie had left her a note telling her that he had taken Pi to the grocery store and they'd be back sometime after three. He also reminded her that today was Sunday and that they would be expected at his mother's for dinner. Great, just what she needed, a day with all the Grants.

Looking around the big kitchen, she decided that she liked it. It was bright and clean and Pi was happy. She was also surprised that there was a gallon of iced tea in the refrigerator. Happier than she expected to be, she poured herself a large glass and sat down at the little table in the alcove. That's when she noticed the answering machine from the other place. Taking it to the study, she plugged it in and started listening. By the time Jamie and Pi returned, she was angry. But enough was enough and she decided that she would handle this on her own.

Markus Lionel was not going to threaten her again. She was finished working with him and she was not making another trip across the country for him. He would have to figure out things on his own. Dane had a house and a boyfriend. Giggling, she wondered how James would feel about being called a "boyfriend."

.

Chapter 18

As soon as the foodstuff was put away and everything cleaned up in the kitchen, Dane told Jamie that she needed to go shopping. She didn't have anything to wear to his mother's house and she wasn't wearing the jeans she'd had on for two days. Pi decided she wanted to stay at the house and play in the yard, which had a surprisingly large herb garden as well as a tilled ground that she would be planting in the spring.

Twenty minutes after walking into the mall, they were walking out. Dane didn't like to shop, had very little experience with it, and knew what she wanted. Next time, though, she was ordering online. She couldn't handle the stress of the people there. And the teller was a horrible person.

"She never stopped chewing her gun. Was there a race or something? Did she hope to make me want to buy more by snapping it every ten seconds? I wanted to smack her in the nose with a rolled up newspaper."

"She's just a kid. You should hear some of the students I have. Last quarter I had this kid who would lean to the side and fart all through class. Not the small, sneaky ones either.

He'd rip one so loud the next class over thought we were having air raid drills."

"You're making that up. Air raid drills indeed. And what was with her flirting with you? I'm standing right next to you and she actually asked you if you wanted her phone number."

Dane was changing in the back of his car. The tinted windows helped, but he kept adjusting his mirror every few miles to try and see her. They were going to get a ticket, she just knew it.

"Yes, well that happens too. What can I say? I'm a cutie. Are you going to change into the bra thingy I picked out? Knowing you have that on is going to make me hard all day. And don't forget Byron's and Ronnie's gift. You think she'll like it?"

"If her husband doesn't kill you first, you mean? What on earth possessed you to buy your sister-in-law a bra and panty set? That's a very personal item." She covered her grin. She had one just like it now and was excited to see his face when she wore it.

"Nah, Devin will love it. And what about what you bought Byr? Chocolate paint and brush set? And how come I couldn't have a set? I'd like to paint you and then eat my way through it." He sounded so cute she almost told him she got him a bigger set with other flavors, but again decided to wait until later.

"Byron was nice enough to show you how to have sex. It's the least I could do for making you one of his best students. Besides, I think Taylor will enjoy it more than he will."

"He did not show me how to have sex. He suggested that I might try something to better my already fantastic ability to have sex. I'm a phenomenal lover." She just grinned at him in the mirror.

They were pulling up in front of the house by then so she didn't answer. Not that she had a lot of experience, but she thought he was better than phenomenal, maybe even the best. Getting out of the car, he pinned her against it. His mouth covered hers before she could say a word. Then it didn't matter, everything else faded away when he touched her.

"You never answered me. I'd like an answer before we go inside. If you give me the right one maybe I won't ravage you standing right here next to the car." He was already making great headway into that. Nibbling at her neck and ears.

Confused, she answered him. "All right, next time we go to the sex shop, you can have a paint set, but I want something too. James, you're making me wet."

His growl echoed through her body and ended in her pussy. She'd be lucky if she didn't have to change clothes again when they got inside. Grinding her body to his, she felt his erection and she wept more.

"Damn it, Dane, will you marry me? I still don't have a ring, but I wanted to pick one out with you. Pi wouldn't even help me, said it was personal between Missy Dane and Mister Jamie — is she going to call me that all the time?"

"Yes." He looked at her strangely and she raised her brow. Now what?

"Yes, you'll marry me or yes she'll call me Mister Jamie all the time?"

"Both. She might be persuaded to call you — put me down, you idiot! What will your family think? You are nuts, did you know that? Swinging me around like a sheet in the wind. I can't believe they let you out at times."

She heard the door behind her open and tried to make herself small behind the car. Jamie pulled her around, rather dragged her around, and shouted up to the group on the porch, "She said yes! She'll marry me."

. "Well of course she did. Come inside before the neighbors call the police again. Idiots. I swear, Dane, I raised him better than this. Come inside." Mrs. Parker waved them in.

Everyone was there. Dane hadn't met Dan or his two grandsons who he and Margaret were raising now. Nor had she met Morgan's twin boys or Ronnie's daughter. Cait was there as well with their new son and Dane was holding him when Devin arrived.

"I just got back from the police department. Thanks to Dane, Phillip Sizemore is now in custody. He's been arrested for the attempt on Jamie's and Dane's lives, mine, and robbery. He also had a multitude of other offences that are too numerous and too boring to name. Thank you, my dear, you are my new best friend. If you ever need anything, just name it and it's yours."

"Good. Then what we discussed last night is a go then. I'm glad. Does this mean you won't charge me now that we're going to be family?"

The discussion about Dane's new wealth was the topic of conversation. Dane and Jamie had discussed what they would do with some of the monies, but if Nick asked, they had a separate plan. And just as Jamie said he would, Nick cornered her before dinner.

"I would like to get my hands on your money, Dane. I can make you so much more than you have now by investing it. The market is a little low right now, but there are opportunities galore if you know where to look."

"Really? I think I've decided to buy an island with it. There's one for sale that I read about in that paper at the end of the grocery aisle where you check out. It says that there isn't any running water or anything and you have to get to it by boat, but I think it'll be fun to make into a resort, don't you? Then there is that charity that was written about there too. Did you know they have a foundation set up that you can have yourself frozen when you die and then thawed out again when they find out the cure? I wonder how that would work if you're shot in the head. What's the matter, Nick, you look sort of, I don't know...green. Doesn't he look green, James?"

"Nicky? Are you all right?"

"A bloody island! Are you insane? Do you know that there is no return rate on that kind of deal? It doesn't even have running water and I won't even go into the fact that it has to be unsanitary and dangerous. And you can't possibly be thinking of investing in cryogenics. My God, woman! You need a keeper!"

The entire room exploded in laughter. Nick took one look around the room then looked back at Dane. "Payback is a bitch, my dear, and I'm good at payback." He jerked her to her feet and kissed her soundly on the mouth. When Jamie growled, he kissed her again.

"Did he put you up to this?" When Dane simply looked over at Devin and Byron, both men took off running, Jamie right behind them. Nick kissed her again and gave chase. Dan saw them coming, opened the door to the back yard for them, and off they went.

Damon got up and followed, taking his medical bag with him, muttering something about tiny brains and big egos. Dane laughed at them all. She sat next to Ronnie, reached under the couch, and handed her the gift.

"This is from James. He said to tell you thanks." When she ripped the paper off, she squealed in delight. "I got me one too." Thinking she needed brownie points with the women more than the men, she handed the other gift to Taylor. Mrs. Parker came in at that time and leaned over Taylor's shoulder to see what it was. Dane went crimson. And when Taylor started explaining what it was for, Dane wished the floor would come up and swallow her.

"I'm curious, that's all," Mrs. Parker said as she picked up a brush. "Taylor has helped my education in this area very nicely. Why, the other day, someone mentioned ball gags and I knew just what he was talking about. It doesn't hurt to be educated, does it, dear?"

"Do we even want to know why you were talking about ball gags with someone?" Morgan asked. Dane was curious, too, but wasn't going to ask.

"No, dear, you do not. Suffice it to say he was quite shocked at my knowledge. Besides, a girl must have some secretes, isn't that right, Morgan?"

The two women glared at each other for several seconds and Dane could feel the emotion thick in the air. No anger, just profound love for each other.

"Oh all right, I'm pregnant again. The boys are two and Nicky and I want to have others. This time, he wants to be there for me and if he doesn't behave, he'll miss this one too. We're hoping for a girl this time."

"It's a girl." Dane hadn't meant to say anything. It just slipped out. When they all turned and looked at her, she heated up again. "I'm sorry. I didn't mean to spoil anything."

Morgan grinned. "Don't tell Nick. Or maybe you could tell him we're having triplets. All boys again. I loved that you got him so well with the money thing. He wouldn't tell me how much, just that you inherited a great deal of money."

"Yeah, eight billion. And some jewelry too. I haven't seen all the paper work yet. You should come out and see the...what?"

"Eight billion? Like in an eight and nine zeros, eight billion? Holy fuck! Can I borrow a couple million?" Morgan asked.

"Sure. I don't need that much money. I mean, who does? That's why I am going to hire your husband. I want to make sure that I can help people like me with it. And James said you head up a charity event every year that helps abused children, Mrs. Parker. I hope you'll let me contribute to it."

"Call me Margaret, dear. Contribute? I'm hoping you, like the rest of my daughters, will help run it. I'm getting old. I need to leave it to others to run. I don't suppose you know how long I have to live, do you? Just kidding. I would love for you to help, love."

"Mrs...Margaret, you will live beyond your years and have a special place in many people's hearts too. My grandmother said you were one of the most influential women she ever met and that you could squeeze a dime out of the tightest politician. She loved working with you and was saddened when you stopped coming to the flower club."

"Good heavens, I hadn't thought of that group of women in years. We should start one. Oh, Dane, what a lovely idea. You'll be in charge. Devin said you have the room at your house. Morgan, you'll be the treasurer; Taylor, you can make sure the members are top notch. Ronnie, you will be the secretary and take the notes at the meetings. Yes, this will be wonderful. I'll spread the word."

The rest of the afternoon was spent planning with Margaret making sure everyone was included in the new club. When Jamie and the other men came in, the only one with a bloodied nose was Damon. He'd gotten knocked over when Devin was tossed over Byron's shoulder.

It was much later than any of them had ever stayed at their mother's, but everyone agreed it was certainly the most entertaining. It was well after three o'clock in the morning when Jamie and Dane returned back to the house. Pi left a note saying that she was calling the utilities in the morning and if she forgot someone, to let her know. Dane looked at the note.

"Do you think we'll get the power turned over to our name or will they think we're invading China? I did it the last time. I'm not so sure she should be in charge of this."

"I'll do it," Jamie said as he took off his shoes. "I have an early class, but I'm free after ten. Let me take it and I'll call them then. Tell her that I wanted to do it. Then tomorrow night, we go ring hunting. Then we'll have dinner. My mother hound you much about a date?"

"Sort of. She wants to wait until the gardens bloom to see if she wants to have it here. I never thought, well, maybe I did, but the gardens here are a show case all summer. Or at least they used to be."

"Good, that'll give us a few months anyway. I'm exhausted, baby. Are you coming to bed? I'm too tired to want to do more than hold you. You've worn me out these past few days."

"No. I can't sleep. I don't usually go to be before eight in the morning. I'll be up by noon if you want to have lunch together. Pi and I are going to see your brother about the money and stuff."

She followed him to their bedroom and lay down next to him. He was so warm and when he pulled her into his arms and snuggled closer, she felt loved. After she was sure he was sound asleep, she got up and went to the pool house.

The building was suitable for what she needed. It was far enough away from the house so that she could get her distance, yet close enough she wouldn't feel unsafe. The windows weren't as long or as wide as she would have liked for them to be, but they could be changed. When she sat on the little wicker chair and looked around, she saw the note.

"*Danish,*

I'm sorry, dear, to leave you all this, but I knew that you would need this house more than anyone else. The money is for you as well. Use it in good health.

I want you to find yourself a good man and get married. Fill this house with lots of children and children's laughter. You're a wonderful woman and I know you'll figure it out. Babies will make you happy, you always made me happy with every smile you gave me. Love, your grandmother."

Dane read it twice more, lay back against the pillow, and closed her eyes. Picking up the book that lay next to her, she rubbed it and felt her grandmother — and her plans for the pool house. Smiling, she sat for a little while longer and went into the house. Her grandmother was the greatest.

Chapter 19

Dane went to the mall first. For as much as she hated it, the early afternoon wasn't as crowed. Besides, they needed linens and other things for the bathrooms. Pi was at the other end buying out the kitchen store. It was just after two when she felt a stir. Before she could turn around, the gun was pointed at her head. She couldn't react quick enough to defend herself.

"Hello, Dane," Markus said softly. "You should have returned my calls. I needed you to help me find some of those people. But now, because of you, I had to kill them. Come along nicely and I won't hurt you too much." She started to raise her hands and he slapped her.

With her arm wrenched behind her back, he led her out of the store and toward his car. She was terrified that he'd find Pi, or worse, Pi would find them. James was still at work and would be for another two hours.

"I'll come with you, but I have to call someone. My boyfriend. I have to call him. He'll come looking for me and then I won't be able to go anywhere."

Dane could feel Markus' insanity. She could also feel that he had indeed murdered some people. She couldn't get a hold on any one person. His mind was jumbled and too hard to see into.

"Boyfriend? Oh no, that won't do. You and I are going to be together for a long time and he'll just get in the way. You should have come to me when I asked, Dane. If I have to hurt him, too, it'll be your fault. We are going to be a team. I'll bring you the stuff and I'll go and find them with your help. I'll be famous." He grinned at that. "The greatest detective in the world, they'll call me. I'll be paid millions to do what you give away."

"Markus, this isn't right. You know that. Someone one will figure—" The slap caught her off guard and nearly threw her to the ground.

"Stupid! Stupid! Stupid! I told you time and time again that people would pay and when you wouldn't...well, someone had to take the money. But when you stopped calling me back and that bitch woman wouldn't give you the phone, I knew it was time to make a change."

She decided to try and be firmer. "I need to call Jamie. I need to tell him that I'm not coming back home. He'll not understand if I don't. Please, Markus, let me call him."

He had shoved her in the back of a van and she slammed her head against one of the walls. She knew she had to stay on her toes or he'd kill her. She wondered how he planned on getting her back on a plane with the gun when he answered her unasked question.

"I had to leave Nevada quick and I decided to settle here. No one knows me but you, and that bitch Pi has never seen me, so I'll be safe. This is because you didn't call me back. It's all your fault, yep, all your fault. I couldn't find that man's bitch of a wife and kid. Anthony Ormond does not like to lose what he thinks of as his." He hit her with his fist again and she had to fight to keep focused. "You call that boyfriend and you tell him that you're not coming home. Tell him you decided not to see him anymore."

"We…he asked me to marry him. I can't just—" The gun hit her this time along the side of her jaw.

"Now look what you've made me do. You need to learn to speak when spoken to." He threatened her again by lunging at her. "I'll tell you what to say and when to say it. Now, you'll call your boyfriend and tell him you want to break it off. You're not going to marry him."

He handed her his cell phone, but she was too dizzy to see the numbers. He jerked it from her hand and dialed what she said. When it started to ring, she prayed she'd be able to convey a message to James without alerting Markus.

"Hello. Grant. How may I help you?"

"Jamie, it's Danish Message. I called to tell you I've decided to call off the wedding."

"Dane? What's going on? What do you mean call off the wedding? Baby, what's happening?"

"Nothing is happening. I've decided that I don't want the ring you gave me after all. I want something closer to what I had before. Mark my words. What you gave me is nothing like I had. I also don't want to have your…I decided that I don't want to carry your kids either. You can find another brood mare to do that shit for you."

"I see. Is there anything else?" His voice sounded so cold it was breaking her heart.

"Yes. Tell Pi she was right all along. Everything she said…all of it was true. And tell her that I love her very much."

"Sure, you break it off with me and tell the housekeeper you love her. That sounds about like you. Well, thanks for telling me. I'll pet the cat for you while I'm at it too, all right?"

"Yes. The cat. I forgot about the cat. I'd like that. It's the least you could do considering."

She closed the phone and her eyes. He got it. She was sure of it. Now she just had to hang on until he found her.

"You are one cold hearted bitch." He stroked her cheek. "Damn, remind me to never get into a pissing contest with you. You are vicious. I love it. You showed more compassion for that damned foreigner and cat than you did him."

This time when he hit her, she couldn't stay afloat. He hit her with his fist again and then her head hit the side of the van. She felt the void rush up to meet her and hoped again James could find her.

~~~

Jamie picked up his landline in his office and called Cait. He wasn't afraid that Spencer would be mad about him calling his wife when she just got home from the hospital. He was more afraid of her anyway. She carried a gun and she knew how to use it. He could shoot as well, but she was better.

"Cait, Dane's been kidnapped. I think I might know who did it, but I have to find Pi. The two of them were headed to the mall this afternoon. If he took her from there, then that's where Pi is."

"Who is it and I'll get an APB out on him." Jamie could have kissed her. "How long ago did it happen? I don't suppose she gave you his name too, did she?"

"I don't know his name, but I'm willing to bet Pi does. Dane said that Pi had been right all along. About everything." Jamie hoped he was right anyway.

"You talked to her? Tell me what she said. Everything, Jamie. Anything she said could be important."

"She said to pet the cat and that she didn't want to wear the ring I got her. She called me Jamie and herself Danish.

And to tell Pi she loved her very much." Jamie closed his eyes. He knew why Dane had said what she did, but it didn't make it hurt any less.

"You have a cat? Why would she want you to pet the cat? Are you sure that's what she said?"

"Cait, I asked her about the cat –you, you're the cat." He wanted to get things going, not explain what she should al… He took a deep breath before continuing. "I was asking her if I should contact you and she said yes to pet the cat for her. And I didn't give her a ring. We were going to the mall to pick it out tonight. I think she was telling me that she was at the mall with him. Keep up, will you?"

"Hey buck-o, I just had a kid." She laughed. "So back the fuck off. And as much as I hate to admit it right now, that was very clever of you two. Stay away from the mall, Jamie. If he sees you there, he might hurt Dane."

"What about Pi? She will freak out if someone tells her she doesn't know that Dane is with this guy. She told me she thinks of Dane as her daughter. I have to tell her, Cait. She'll get hysterical if I don't do it."

"Damn it. Call your mom. Tell her what's going on. This is just what I need, your mother and a woman who barely speaks English in a mall full of people, flipping out. I can see the headlines now. 'Crazed Chinese Woman and Head of Children Services Have Screaming Fit in Mall, more at eleven.' Tell Margaret to remain calm and bring Pi out the food court exit. I'll have a plain car waiting there to bring her to you." Cait drew a loud, deep breath. "We'll get her, Jamie. Don't worry."

He called his mother next. Cait must have called Spencer because while Jamie was still trying to calm his mother down, Spencer burst into his office. He knew that he was talking to another brother; his cell was plastered to his head.

"Yes, Mom. Please, just tell her whatever you need to get her out of the mall without causing a scene." Jamie rubbed his aching forehead. "I'll tell her when I see her. Dane isn't stupid. She'll get us to her."

"Well of course she isn't stupid. What a thing to say. Did this man kidnap her because of her money? He worked fast if he did. That poor child. When you get her back, you tell her I love her, all right, Jamie?" He heard her turn off the car. "I'm at the mall. I'm betting she's at the kitchen place. That woman has probably bought out half the store. Hopefully they won't mind holding it for her. Maybe I can make arrangements to have it delivered to your new home. What do you think?"

"Mom, I love you, but I don't give a rat's ass about the stuff she's bought. I want my Dane back." He closed his eyes. "I'm sorry. I know you're trying to help. I'm worried. She's my life. I can't...I'm sorry."

"You're a little too tall for me to wash your mouth out with soap. But I'll think of something." Her laugh made him smile. "Oh dear, Jamie, she has bought out the store. She has a cart that the construction people use to cart around brick and stuff. I'll call you back when we leave."

As soon as he hung up, his phone rang again. It was Ronnie. She and Devin were on their way to pick him up, he was not to drive. Jamie looked up at Spencer, who was still on his phone to whoever.

"I want to go to our house," he told Ronnie. "Mom is going to bring Pi there. She'll want to cook, it calms her. Can you call the rest of the family and let them know that's where I'll be if they need me? They don't have to come, but they should know where I am."

Ronnie snorted. "Like you'd be able to keep us away. I'll text everyone with your location now. And Pi will need more food. I'll call a friend of mine who owns an upscale store and have him bring out the works. Do you mind if the kids and nannies come too? That way we can stay together."

"No, one thing we have is plenty of room. I'd like the family with me. Ronnie, I can't…I need her back. I don't think I can…she's my life." He didn't know why he kept telling people that, but it did calm him somewhat.

"She'll be home soon and be spitting mad that all this fuss was made over it. And Jamie, you've got the best working at getting her back. Cait won't let anything happen to her." He knew that too.

Spencer was pacing again. He did that when he was nervous. When he noticed that Jamie wasn't talking, he sat down.

"Cait will find her and bring her home. She said to tell you she loves you. Meggie is coming here too. Did I hear you right? Are we going to the big new digs?"

"Yeah, Mom is picking Pi up now." Jamie put his head in his hands before he continued. "Then we'll all meet at the house. Ronnie is having more food brought in. You know this is a lot of people for Pi. I think she'll be all right though. She loves Dane. And Dane loves her."

"Mom says she's a hoot. I'll ride over with you and Devin. He called to tell me what was going on. Taylor is closing down the office. Byron is catching a flight home from Germany. He said he'd catch a taxi there. Nick and Morgan are leaving as soon as they pick the twins up at preschool, and Dan and the boys are picking up Damon at the hospital. He is bringing his kit. He also said to tell you that he had a date tonight and you owe him big time." Spencer leaned back in his chair. "He said that he wants a paint by number kit too. Want to explain that to me?"

Devin walked in the door just as he was finishing up the story behind the chocolate and brushes. It seemed that everyone wanted a set for Christmas or their birthday, whichever came the soonest. Jamie told them he was getting one first.

The drive to the house was long; Jamie just wanted to find Dane and make love to her and pretend none of this had happened. And he needed to talk to Pi. Jamie just hoped she was easy to make understand and that he could understand her. He was beginning to love the batty woman and didn't want to have to strangle her. He sat her down in the kitchen with his family around and a couple of men who had come with Cait. Men with nice suits and guns under their arms.

"You tell me what happen to Missy Dane or I hex your twig and berries. Missy Dane be mad, but you make me wait long enough. Split it now, Mister Jamie. I worried."

"Someone has kidnapped her." Jamie took Pi's hands into his. "Dane said to tell you she loved you and that you were right. Do you know what she meant?"

"She tell you how much she love Pi?" That made her smile then she frowned. "She said anything else? I need to know. It important."

"Dane said to tell you she loves you very much and that you were right all along and that you were right about everything. Does that help?"

"It be that bastard Markus. He a weasel of bad kind. He make her sick before. I tell her that he bad man, she no listen. Now we cut his wiener off and make it roast over fire then serve it to him. I no like him."

No kidding, Jamie thought. He found himself cupping his groin and hoping never to make Pi this upset with him. He looked at his brothers, who were trying not to do the same thing. Cait snorted at them and turned to Pi. Easy for her to say. A man's "wiener" was all he had.

"Pi?" Cait asked her. "What's his last name, and do you have a picture of him? I want to find him too and you and I will discuss his demise. Also, how did he make Dane sick before?"

"His name is...train, Miss Dane say. Like a train. He make her sick by making her keep going. It hard for her. No time to rest. He keep sending her stuff to look at. She tell him no more. I heard her, she say he have to learn to do job himself. You want hear it?"

"Hear it? Yes, I'd like to...train, you mean like the railroad company?" Cait looked at Jamie and he shrugged. He didn't know. "Or a toy? Can you remember anything else?"

Cait followed her into the study, Jamie close behind. He liked this room and wondered if Dane would let him set up his office in here. The smell of cigar smoke made him think of his father and grandfather. Pi walked over to the answering machine and pushed the button.

A man's voice was leaving a message wanting Dane to call him back immediately. Then Dane answered him. Jamie watched as two men from Cait's office started taking notes. He read their notes as they wrote.

Chapter 20

Dane woke to a dark room. The only bit of light was from beneath the door that was just in front of her. She was tied up, her arms up over her head, and she was hanging from them. Her feet were on the floor, but just barely. Every time she tried to move, the rope would cut into her wrists. The gag on her mouth cut into her mouth and lips.

The room wasn't very big, she could feel that, and she could also feel the others that had been in here, their despair, the pain and the terror. Death was here, all through the room, and even on the gag in her mouth. She tried screaming, but she couldn't make a noise past the cloth. Terror made sweat bead on her skin and she could feel it dripping down her back.

Trying to focus on building a wall around her mind, she kept listening to anything that might tell her where she was and if help was available. The room was too loud and the voices of emotion too strong. Her mind simply shut down and she slipped back into darkness.

The next time she opened her eyes, Markus was sitting in a chair in front of her. There was also more light this time. He looked pleased with himself and he had a single red rose in his hand. When he noticed Dane was awake, he stood and brought the rose to her cheek and ran it down to her chin. She tried not to pull away, but he must have seen something and slapped her again. She simply let the darkness take her away.

Keeping her eyes closed this time, she reached out into the room to see if she was alone. Her head hurt so bad that she couldn't concentrate long, but it was enough to let her know no one living was with her this time. Opening her eyes, she could see that the light under the door was brighter and that she could smell something, some sort of food smell wafting through the air. The odor made her belly jump and she thought she might throw up. Terrified she would kill herself if she did throw up with the gag in her mouth, she tried to breathe through all of it. She took several deep breaths into her nose and tried to think of anything else.

James. He would come for her. Dane knew he would, and Cait would too. They would find her and she would be all right. She had to keep saying that to herself. She couldn't lose hope. When a shadow crossed over the front of the door, she closed her eyes and relaxed against the rope. When the door lock was clicked and the brightness of the outer room shone against her eyes, Dane knew the door had been opened. She reached out gently and found Markus and a man she didn't think she knew. But something was…familiar to her.

"See, I told you I had her. You just need to give me a little more time to acclimate her to my way of doing things. She'll find your wife and child. I had to hit her a couple of times to get her to listen, but she'll be ready to work when she wakes up."

~~~

He sounded so calm, so normal that Dane could almost believe that he was the same Markus she knew. The one who she had worked with all those years.

188

"Ain't nothing wrong with hitting a woman to keep her in line. You remember that. And I don't give a turd's hell about that brat. I want that woman back. She's mine and I mean to have her. Nothing gets away from me, unlessin' I say it can. Don't know who helped her, but I wanna know that too. Got me some lessons to teach when she comes back. You and that girl there will make sure I get her too or else'n I'm gonna make you sorry you were born. Got me, boy?"

"Oh yes, Mr. Ormond. Dane and I are a team now. We'll deliver. Don't you worry about at thing." Markus' voice sounded slightly afraid and she could feel his fear of the other man too.

Dane waited until she heard the lock click before she opened her eyes. An urge to giggle caught in her throat. They actually locked the door and she was tied up like a Thanksgiving turkey. Did they expect her to cut herself down and then get away? she wondered. The room was screaming at her again and it was beating at her mind like a thousand little knives. She needed to get out of here or she would shut down. And she doubted that Markus would be calling Pi for instructions on how to wake her. Working at building the wall, she tried to concentrate. But pain was taking its toll on her too. She needed to work harder, she realized, before she went somewhere she couldn't return from without help.

When Markus came in later, Dane was fighting the demons. She could feel eight different tragedies in this room. There were no windows and he had painted the walls flat black; the smell of fresh paint stung her nose. Her arms ached and she was pretty sure she was bleeding from somewhere on her face. The blood was dripping onto her chest and spilling down her shirt. Using every bit of her energy, she focused on Markus and what he was saying.

"You'll do as you're told, Dane, or I will punish you." He snarled at her. "I know what to do to keep you in line. Your mother did it to you and look what happened. I'll start out slow for you. I know I hit you too hard, but you must learn to listen."

He put a cloth next to her face. It was too close to see, but she could smell the blood all over it. She tried to jerk away from it, but she couldn't move. Screaming behind the gag, she reached for anyone she could touch and begged for help. When the cloth touched her face, she lost consciousness.

The cold water brought her awake screaming. It was only a small amount, probably just enough to fill a glass, but she wasn't so deep yet that it wouldn't work to bring her around. The first thing she noticed was that her shirt was gone and the second, there was someone else in the room with her besides Markus. He was sane...sort of, but he was evil. And she did know him. The moment she realized who he was, she began to scream behind the gag and struggle to get away.

"Ah Dane, decided to join us did you? Good. This will be you're first lesson in learning to obey me. I guess you know who this is, don't you. Remember? He helped your mommy all those years ago right before you disappeared. It took me forever to find him. But he's been so busy since those days. It seems he's developed quite a taste for the whip. Haven't you, Carl?" Markus' laughter made her sick. "I'm going to leave you two alone to get reacquainted."

Dane started screaming again the moment the door closed behind Markus. Carl moved up behind her and started touching her with something. Her body reacted to the contact by convulsing and jerking. The power of the emotions on it ripped through her mind and body like a freight train. Death. So much death. He'd killed so many with this whip.

"You were such a willful child." His voice was so soft and low. "Your mother paid me so much money to hurt you. I wanted to tell her I'd do it for free, but I like spending the money on whores and drink. Makes me horny to hit, to make someone bleed. I'm going to put a matching set of scars on your back, baby girl. You're going to remember me every time you look in the mirror. And Markus don't care none. He don't wanna fuck you, he said. He said so long as I don't hurt your head, I could have as much fun as I wanted."

The first slap of the whip took her breath away. His laughter tore at her memories and she tried to slide into a light place that she went when the world around her got to be too much. She was too weak, the loss of blood, the room, and the bombardment of it proved too much. By the time Carl had delivered his tenth blow to her back, Dane had slipped into a deep hole. And unless she got help soon, no amount of water was bringing her back. And she was at the point by then that she didn't care.

~~~

Jamie read the notes from the answering machine. They were verbatim and they were precise.

Man: "Dane, if you're there, answer the fucking phone. I've had enough of this. I need you to help me find a woman and her child."

Danish: "I'm here. Markus I can't do this anymore. I've had enough. I've had the week from hell and I—"

Man: "What's happened? I haven't heard from you all week and now you're telling me you're done. I'm afraid I can't let that happen, Dane. I've a great many people depending on me."

Danish: "Depending on you? How on earth are they depending on you? I thought your team knew about me. You said they all worked hard on keeping me out of the media. Are you taking credit for what I've been doing?"

Man: "Are you kidding? I'd have to share the proceeds if I did that. No, baby, it's all you and me. We are going to clean up the streets with your power and my smarts."

Danish: "I've never charged a single person for my help. I told you that. But you have, haven't you? You've been charging for my help and taking the money. Christ, I've been doing this for eight years, paying for my own plane fare to come to you, and you've been making a profit? How dare you?"

Man: "Damn right I dare. I dare a great many things. You'd be well to remember that, Swedish Danish Messenger. Yeah, I know all about your mother and her methods to control you. The way she would lock you in that dark room until you begged to come out. Well, I've got my own little dark room just waiting for you. And if I have to come for you, you'll be very sorry."

Danish: "Fuck you, Markus. You come near me and I will kill you."

Phone disconnects.

"This is a long enough call that we could trace it, but it's a cell phone. He did call her from here somewhere in Ohio. It was about ten miles from where she lived when she received it. But that was five days ago. If he has her, and I've no doubt that he does, it'll have to be in a place that will be secluded. He talks about a dark room. Do you know what that might be, Mr. Grant?"

Jamie looked up from the transcript of the call. He had to ask the officer to repeat it. This man had his Dane.

"No, I'm sorry, but Pi might know. She and Dane have been friends for a very long time. Let me get her for you."

Jamie walked into the kitchen and looked around. There was food everywhere. Sandwiches and pies, cakes, and a pot roast. There were Chinese dumplings and French fries, pancakes, and bacon. He could see one of the ovens was on and it looked like a whole turkey was in there. The stove was covered in pans, potatoes boiled in one, carrots in another. Rice was steaming on the back burner and there were chopped up vegetables in a large wok steaming. Along the counter under the window were gallons of tea, some with sugar, some without. A large coffee urn brewed in the corner and several cups along with cream, sugar, and spoons rested on a tray. But he didn't see Pi. When he went to look in the pantry, he saw her outside with Morgan and the boys. He walked out to talk to her.

"Hello, Jamie," Morgan said as she walked toward him. "We were just taking a break. Pi has been busy. We were just discussing the merits of inviting everyone here next Sunday. Your mother is fine with it so long as Pi cooks less food."

"I go overtop, Mister Jamie. I cook when I tinsel. Missy Dane said it good thing I not have too much." Her smile was sad. "She come back she be pissyed at me, I think. I don't care, but she be there."

"I have to agree. It's not good to have too much tinsel. The police have a few questions for you, Pi. That man said he—"

"Lionel!" she said suddenly. "That it. The train. Missy Dane call him that too, freighter train. His name is Markus Lionel. I knew I'd rethink it. That help, Mister Jamie?"

They all ran into the house and began talking at once. It took Cait a few seconds to catch up with them, but once she did, she called someone to do a search on him. When that didn't turn up anything, Pi looked crushed. Jamie pulled her into his arms and held her again as she cried.

"Try it backwards. I mean, they're both first and last names. Maybe he just turned it around," Byron suggested with a shrug.

"Bingo!" Cait smiled. "Two hits on an M. Lionel. He rented a van the day before yesterday and he's rented a house on Broad Street. I'll get my men there in ten minutes. I'm going too. Saddle up, boys, we're going to have some fun."

"Uhhh, O'Malley, you aren't going anywhere. You just had a baby less than five days ago, by C-section I might add. And I nearly lost you. I can't…you aren't even supposed to be up and around this much." Spencer looked ready to do battle. So did Cait.

"Spencer, I have to go. I'm alive because she told you I would be. I'm here because she said that she saw us holding our son. I can't fail this woman again. I need to be there. I can't sit on the sidelines again, not now that she's going to be a part of my family."

Jamie didn't know what to say. He wanted Cait to stay home too, but he wasn't going to stay home either. He had to find his Dane and he figured Cait felt the same way. Jamie didn't ask nor did he comment when the FBI agent raised his brow at him. He simply kissed his mother, slipped on his coat, and went to one of the many vehicles that were being loaded. Pi came out to speak to him.

"Missy Dane need you to touch her," she told him softly. "She will need good touches, not hard. You don't let nobody touch her who not love her. Tell her I have house ready when she come here."

"I will, Pi. And thank you. I'm so glad that you're here for us. We are both going to need you so much when we get settled." Jamie kissed her cheek. "We're going to make you a grandma. You're staying right here with us."

"I not going nowhere. I be here. You just bring my Missy Dane home, Mister Jamie. Bring her back here to me."

By the time they left, there were nearly twenty more men with them. Vests that said POLICE, SWAT, and FBI were all around them. There were SUVs, vans, and large vehicles, Jamie had no idea what they were. There was even an ambulance and a medical team on standby.

~~~

The house was situated just where they thought it would be. Deep into the woods and no neighbors for miles. There was a single car out front that had been leased to an M. Lionel, and the house was lit up. Jamie and Cait were told to stay in the SUV until someone came back to get them. The men had silently left the vehicles and had fanned out over the area as silent as the wind.

As soon as they were out of sight, Cait reached behind them into the back of the seat and handed him a vest. He looked at her. The letters POLICE were bold across the back and the front. She started putting hers on.

"I'm not sitting here when she needs us," she told him when he just sat there. "You can come or go, but if you go, you go hot, understand me? You fire to the chest if you have to. No more head shots for you. The last time you were damned lucky you didn't kill anyone else or miss."

"I didn't though. And I'll agree I was lucky. Both of us were. And bite me, girl. I saved Ta's life."

He pulled off his coat, slipped the vest over his head, and Cait helped him secure it. When he was buckled up, he reached behind him and pulled his gun, a Glock nine millimeter, out and racked one in the chamber. Satisfied, they both quietly left the car and moved to the house.

As they made their way to the house, staying behind the men who were going to hit the house first, Jamie thought about the last time he'd pulled his gun out for something other than target practice. Taylor had been in trouble and he'd killed a man.

She had been hurt by a man who she worked for. He and his brother, the law firm of Freedom Fighters of all things had been using Taylor as a fall guy in a huge multimillion dollar insurance scam. While visiting her in the hospital, Paul Freedom had come into her room and demanded that she tell him where his money was. When he fired at Taylor, Jamie fired too, and had killed him with a single gunshot wound to the head.

One of the men directly in front of them suddenly stopped and turned back to Cait and Jamie. Neither he nor Cait were under any delusions that the unit they were following didn't know they were there. They had to have known from the beginning that they'd follow. He was talking in a headset when he started for them.

"They found the woman. The house is secure. They want you both in there now."

Jamie took off running. All he could think about was that he'd said they found the woman, not they had found a body. He knew deep down that it could be either way, but he couldn't think that she was dead. Not now, not now that they had found each other.

Chapter 21

An officer nearly tackled Jamie as he came barreling into the room. If Cait hadn't been behind him, he would probably have been hauled off to jail. As it was, he was escorted down to the basement by the guy who kept giving him an odd look. The door was blocked when he and Cait got to the bottom.

"We haven't touched her except to feel for a pulse. We were told by her physician that under no circumstances were we to touch her unless it was life or death. We've contacted him and he is going to meet us at the hospital. Life flight is on their way. ETA is about three minutes." He waited a few seconds before he continued. "Sir, she's been beaten and her breathing is shallow. Her pulse is weak but steady. If we can't get her to respond, we will have to try something soon."

Jamie nodded. Beaten. Weak pulse. Shallow breathing. Life flight. He looked over at Cait, who nodded at him. When the medic moved, Jamie walked in.

Dane was still hanging from the ceiling, her shirt and bra missing. Jamie took off his coat and wrapped it around her. She was so cold, worse than she had been before. He looked over at the officer standing there with his gun pointed to the floor as he watched the room. No one was looking at Dane. Be he could see that they were concerned.

"Do you have a knife?" The agent next to him nodded and looked relieved. "We'll need to cut her down. And do you think you can have someone bring us a blanket?"

Jamie didn't know where the calm was coming from, but he was glad for it. While the agent sawed through the ropes, he and Cait held her between them. Cait was crying, he saw. Jamie refused to think beyond what he was doing.

As soon as Dane was loose, her body dropped limply in his arms and he held her to him. When the blanket arrived, he wrapped her up in it and carried her up the stairs. Her arms and legs swung with each step he took. When he got her to the kitchen and then outside, he rocked her gently in his arms. Someone, he assumed Cait, kept telling him that Dane would be fine. Then he heard the whop-whop of the chopper.

They wouldn't let him ride with her. He nearly drew his gun and shot the man to make him understand how serious it was when a squawk of a radio pierced the night. The medic stepped away and an armed agent stepped in front of Jamie. He wondered briefly if he had orders to shoot him if he tried to touch the medic.

"He goes," the medic said when he came back, and pointed at Jamie. "Not the detective. I don't know who you know, but someone wants you on this thing. If you get in my way, I'll throw you from the fucking chopper myself. Get in the front and don't say a fucking word."

Jamie decided he could live with that. But before he could move, he felt a sting hit him in the leg and he fell. His first thought was that the agent really had shot him. Then he realized that the agent was holding him down with a knee in his back. Cait was shouting, but he couldn't understand her either. Things got fuzzy after that. But he could swear he saw flames come from Cait's hands. As he was fading out, he realized that she was shooting at something.

Jamie woke up in the ambulance. He tried to sit up, but was pushed back down with a firm hand. The woman sitting next to him looked like she could beat bear with a switch, as his grandfather used to say. He decided he might just ask his questions from the prone position.

"Dane? Where is Dane? And Cait, my sister-in-law. If I let anything happen to her, my brother will never forgive me."

"The woman in the chopper is in the air," she told him as she checked his eyes with a spotlight. "Nothing has changed with her status. Detective Grant? She's filling out a report last I heard and stripping the hide off every agent on the ground. I wouldn't want to work for her. She has a very low tolerance for mistakes, doesn't she?"

Jamie didn't point out that he was in an ambulance and because they had told them the area was secure. He also didn't want to point out that Cait had just had a kid a few days ago and had been shot at as well. No, he wanted to make it there in one piece. A phone ringing behind him had him turn but not sit up. He wasn't that far gone yet.

"There's a woman on the phone. She says she's your mother and if you're hurt she's going to kick your ass. Her words, not mine. Wanna talk to her?"

He took the phone from the man offering it to him and listened as his mother ranted. She didn't know he had been handed the phone and was still giving the driver a piece of her mind. He had to smile. The next time she fussed at them for their language, he was going to bust her.

"Wow, such language. You kiss your kids with that mouth?" he asked her when it sounded like she was taking a breath to continue.

"Jamie? Oh baby, are you all right? They told us you'd been shot. Are you shot?" She was crying now and he wanted to assure her.

"Honestly, Mom, I don't know what happened. I'm assuming that I was. They have my pants cut off my leg and I can see blood on the padding. I'm not feeling like I'm in pain."

"Shock. Tell her you're in shock. It'll wear off soon and you'll hurt like a mother fucker." She smiled like she was waiting for it to hit him. "You took a bullet to the left thigh. The bullet is still in there, but a surgeon is on standby when we get there," the medic, Carol, said as she filled out something on a clip board.

"Did you hear that, Mom?" She said she had. "Are you there at the hospital? Has Dane got there yet?"

"Yes, I'm here now and no, not yet. They said ETA forty seconds—how do they do that. Forty seconds? Cait said she'd been beaten again. Oh, Jamie, that poor girl. Pi is with me. I didn't want to leave her alone. She's taking it very hard. She wants to see you both. I told everyone she's Dane's mother. I hope that's all right."

"Of course. And she is." And Jamie loved his mom all the more for thinking of Pi at a time like this. "Stay with Dane, Mom. I don't want anyone to…I love her and I don't want her to hurt anymore. She has to be…I need her to be all right."

"I know you do, son. I won't leave her side." Jamie heard someone speaking before she continued. "Damon can't treat you until you have the bullet removed. Cait is on her way in. Spencer is fit to be tied. She killed him, though. Cait killed that Lionel person when he shot at you."

Jamie remembered the fire now and Cait shouting. He couldn't talk anymore. The "mother fucking" pain hit him hard. Thankfully, it took him into a black hole where it didn't hurt so badly.

The next time he woke, Damon was in the room with him. His knee was propped up on a pillow and a harness was holding it up at the foot. His pain was sort of fuzzy, but he could tolerate it.

"How's Dane? Can I see her?" Damon jerked as though he'd been asleep and Jamie smiled. No rest for the weary.

"She's in intensive care," he said as he sat up. "They operated on her back and had to do quite a bit of removal of the old scar tissue. She'll be sore, but she'll not have those reminders anymore. A plastic surgeon was called in to do the work. She still hasn't woken yet. Pi hasn't left either of your sides for no more than it takes to go from one room to another. I've already cleared it to have you moved to her. Pi seems to think Dane just needs to be loved."

"When can I go? I need to see her." Damon looked...odd. He started to ask him, but his mother burst into the room.

"Oh thank goodness. I swear if one more of my sons get hurt, I'm putting you all in a padded room and posting a guard outside the room. How are you doing, baby?"

"Fine. Sore. Damon was just taking me to see Dane." It took half an hour to get him rolled down the hall and another ten minutes to set him up. He was exhausted and in pain. But before he would let them give him anything, he had to touch her.

They had her lying on her back and there were all sorts of tubes running along her. She had two IV's in her hand and he could hear the slow but steady beep-beep of another machine. She looked so pale and her lips were dry, lips he wanted desperately to kiss. Damon had pushed him close enough to touch her and that's what he did now.

Her skin was cool, but not cold like it had been. He could feel her pulse beating beneath her skin at her wrist. He lifted it to his mouth and kissed it. Then held it to his cheek.

"Missy Dane very deep this time. Man make her go to her place. She need some way to find her way home."

Jamie looked up at Pi. He'd forgotten she was here. Looking at her, he realized she was exhausted and worn. But he knew that telling her to leave would break her heart even if he could convince her to do it.

"Has she ever been this deep before?" She shook her head then frowned. He knew she was trying to remember.

"One time maybe. She say she lost. I not able to help her find way back. You help her, Mister Jamie. Bring in good touch. She find way home when Granny bring her good touch."

Good touch. She had said that to him before. Don't let anyone touch her that didn't have a good touch. Jamie held Dane's hand and tried to think what she meant when Cait walked in with Paddy.

"I brought you some lunch. And don't you dare tell me that you're not hungry. If you want to watch Paddy when…why are you looking at me like I've got a steak around my neck?"

"Oh, Caitlynne Grant, I think I might have to kiss you. Bring me Paddy. Call Mom, have her and Dan bring Jacob and little Jim. Meggie too. I'll call Nick and have him bring the twins. We need some good touches and they are just the ones to bring it."

~~~

She was hot. Not just hot, but roasting hot. When Dane tried to move away from the heat, it grunted. Did heat grunt? She tried again and it screamed at her.

"If you would just open your flipping eyes, I'll move him. Otherwise, he stays right where he is. I swear if he doesn't sleep in his own bed after this, I'm killing your future husband." Cait?

It was an effort, but she got one eye open and immediately closed it. Pain shot through her head like a knife. She felt the light dim and she tried again.

"Sorry about the lights. Paddy needed his diaper changed and I'm so not doing that in the dark again. Did you know that boys can pee in your face when you take off their diaper? Disgusting. If I didn't love him so much already, I'd sell him. How are you feeling?"

Her mouth was dry and thick. Her tongue felt as if a trash truck was using is as a dump site. She ached in places she couldn't remember having a body part for and she still couldn't move.

"Hot. Dry." It took her four tries to say that and she could only hope she made sense.

"Damon said you could have some ice chips but nothing more. I don't know why they don't just let you have a drink of water, same difference. I have to call the nurse so she can alert the troops. Jamie is going to be pissed. I just sent him to the house to shower. He was sort of rank."

"Too many words. Shhhh…" She felt herself slip away again.

When she opened her eyes the next time, she wasn't as hot, but she still hurt. There wasn't anyone in front of her, but she could hear someone talking behind her. The thought of turning her head seemed too much effort so she tried to lift her hand. That's when she looked down. There was a kid there—a little one, but a kid. That can't be right.

"Cait?" Her voice sounded harsh and it hurt her throat to talk. She really wanted some of those ice chips she could see on the half table, but couldn't make her tongue move to ask.

"Hey, baby. How are you? Let me get you some ice." Heaven entered her mouth in the form of a plastic spoon of cold water. And her James was giving it to her.

"Where…where am I?" Closing her eyes again, she had to fight to keep awake, but she wasn't winning. She wanted to talk to James, but she couldn't seem to keep her eyes open.

The little girl in front of her waved and smiled when she opened her eyes next. Dane was beginning to think the world had been taken over by shrimps. That thought made her giggle, which hurt. She looked down at her arm and was relieved to see that there didn't seem to be anything in the crook of her arm this time.

"Ice?" Meggie, this little girl, was Spencer's and Cait's. When she frowned at Dane, she remembered that she was deaf and tried looking at the cup on the table. Someone moved into her peripheral vision and she saw James again.

"Hi. Are you going to stay with me this time? I want to tell you I love you in case you fade again. Are you in any pain?"

"No. Not bad." Her throat almost felt normal and she could move her hands. Her back felt tight, but she could move more. "Can't remember."

"Damon said for you to take it easy in trying to do that. He said that you may have a little memory, loss but it'll be temporary at most. What do you remember?"

"Markus took me. I talked to…talked to you. Cait was here with baby. Pi. Is Pi all right? She is protective." She wasn't tired, but the light hurt. "Lights off, please?"

"Yes, of course." The dimness felt better.

"Pi?"

"She's at home now. We had to send her home for a little while. She was dizzy from lack of sleep. I told her she wouldn't do you any good if she was in the hospital too. She said she'd be back tonight. Did you know that she is afraid to ride in a car but will ride in a taxi? Anyway, I offered to pick her up, but she is coming and going with a service that I've arranged."

"She was in the front seat of a car that rolled and ended up in the river when she was a child. She thinks if she's in the back, she'll be fine. I'm the only person she'll ride with unless it's an emergency. Thank you."

"I love you. My family is waiting to come in and see you. Meggie went to tell them that you're awake. Is it all right if they come in? I won't let them stay long."

"I need to brush my teeth. Can I do that first? My mouth feels like a dumpster. And can I roll over? I feel heavy."

He looked away from her and she almost asked. But he picked up the water and showed her a toothbrush and she forgot. It took them ten minutes to brush her teeth twice and rinse. She was exhausted again when they were done.

His family crowded in the room and each of them came to stand next to the bed to see her. She didn't ask again to roll over; there was something there just out of reach that she should know. When Cait laid Paddy next to her again, she pulled him close and fell asleep.

The dream started with her arms tied up over her head. She was crying and begging one minute then she was gagged the next. Incredible pain ripped through her back. She could feel her skin tear and the whip lashed across her skin. Wood under her feet hurt her. She could feel splinters imbed into her, but then the cold of concrete would make her ache with pain. Markus then Carl, then Markus again, their faces interchangeable and merging into one. The laughter, the screaming, all of it raced over her and through her, ending in a scream so real so loud that she woke herself up.

"Dane! Dane, listen to me. It's a dream, baby. Hear me? It's a dream. I have you. You're safe. It's a dream."

"James?" It was fading, the dream, the smells. She could see the room they were in, James in the bed with her, Pi standing close, holding her hand.

"Yes, baby. I'm here. Pi is too. It was a dream. It's over, I have you. We have you."

Her heart was pounding and she could smell the sweat on her body. Terror was fading from her and she snuggled closer to the man holding her.

"Missy Dane you scared me. You be fine. I have you now. You be fine with Pi and Mister Jamie." Dane pulled her hand into hers and kissed it. She went to sleep knowing that she was safe.

Chapter 22

Jamie was still asleep when she woke up again. Looking around her hospital room, she wondered where such a big bed came from that two people could lie in it. When the door opened, she looked up to see Margaret.

"Hello, darling. You feeling better this morning?" she whispered. Margaret took her hand.

"I remembered last night. That's why I can't roll to my back. He beat me again, didn't he?"

"Yes, but it's not the reason you can't roll over. They did some reconstructive surgery on you and the repair work was very extensive. They had to remove a great deal of scar tissue from your back. Damon thinks you'll be able to sit up today. It'll only be for short periods at first, but you'll be fine in a few weeks."

"I knew the man who hit me. Both of them really, but the man with the whip, he was the one who beat me when I was a teenager. I don't know how Markus found him, but he did."

"He knew him through your mother. Markus' real name is Peter Market. He has been pulling one scam after another since he was a kid. You were just the biggest catch. Market contacted your mother right after the article came out about your mental health issues and that you would be out of circulation for an extended period of time. He was going to write an article on you. She, of course, had a different spin on things and that's how he got the idea to contact you." James kissed her nose when she turned to look at him as he continued. "Market is dead. Cait killed him when he shot me. I'm all right, just need to be on crutches for a few more weeks."

"I don't remember that. When Carl hit me with the whip, I zoned out. I had to or the room was going to kill me. There were...someone murdered people, children, down there. I couldn't get a reading on Markus, err, Market, because of his insanity, but Carl was there too. They told me that he had acquired a taste for the whip after me."

Dane shuddered and reached for Jamie's hand. He laced his fingers with hers and held her. His kiss was soft but full of so much love she felt the tears fall down her cheeks.

"I love you, Dane. You're all right now, okay? I was so worried about you. Don't do that again. I can't be shot anymore or my mom is going to put me away." Dane heard the faint click of the door and knew they were alone.

"I'll try. Are you really all right? I don't want you to hurt because of me." She pressed her head against his shoulder and breathed in. He smelled so good to her, warm and masculine, soft and hard.

"I'm fine. Better now that you can stay awake for more than five minutes." This kiss was warmer, stronger than the last, and when he brushed his mouth over hers again, she opened for him and groaned at the first sweep of his tongue as it moved along hers. When Jamie cupped her head and deepened the kiss, she felt like she had come home. A throat clearing brought them back before they could go much further.

"I'm sorry. I hate to interrupt—"

"Then go away. I was kissing my future wife. And I'd like to take up where you made me leave off."

"Doctor Wallace? I'm Agent Brownville. I need to just ask you a couple of questions to finish things off. We've gotten most of it from Mr. Grant here and the local police, but there are just one or two I think only you can help with."

The door opened and in walked Damon and two nurses. He leaned over and kissed Dane on the forehead and winked at James. Dane thought Damon looked odd, but didn't say anything.

"I'm sorry, agent, but I'll have to ask you to step out for a moment. We need to get Dr. Wallace out of bed for the first time and I have the time right now to do it. We won't be a moment." The agent was out the door, Dane thought, before he knew what hit him.

"What are you up to? You couldn't wait ten minutes? I want him to stop stalking the halls waiting for Dane to wake up. Let him finish this—"

"Devin wants her to have her lawyer present. And Cait is coming in too. But I do want to get you up, my dear. Jamie, do you want to stay or leave? It's going to be painful for her."

"I'm staying. But you hurt her too much and I'll return the favor. I may be injured, but not forever."

Dane might have laughed, but she was worried how bad it was going to hurt too. The nurses helped Jamie out of her bed and into one of the easy chairs. When he was settled, they came back to help her.

"Okay, sweetheart, this is what we're going to do. We are going to roll you over and sit you up at the same time. It will stretch your back and hurt like hell, but I don't want you to do anything but move with us. Sandy is going to take one shoulder and I'm going to take the other. When you're over to your side, Tammy is going to take your legs and roll with us so that you're sitting up. All right? We won't stop if you yell. It's going to hurt anyway so we should just get it over with. Jamie, don't move from that chair. If I have to tie you down, tell me now. She's going to hurt, deal with it."

Dane took several deep breaths and when she nodded to Damon, she was over and up in seconds. The scream ripping from her throat lasted longer. It took her several more seconds to hear what Damon was saying.

"Deep breaths, honey. That's it. Breathe through your nose and out your mouth. Keep breathing. I promise it'll pass; in your nose, out your mouth."

She sat there for a full five minutes just breathing. Every once in a while, Damon would ask Jamie if he was okay, and when he answered he was, he'd talk her through breathing again.

"I'm okay. I'm better. Dizzy, but better. Now what?"

"Now the hard part." She nearly hit him. She might have, too, if she didn't think it would hurt so badly. "You're going to walk to the chair and sit down. I know this will hurt, but not as bad as moving you over. We need to get you up and about. The sooner you're moving, the better you'll feel."

The room spun around and she felt herself sway when she finally stood, but she was upright. After the first two or three steps, it got easier too. The pull in her back was painful, but he was right; she did feel better just moving again. Ten minutes to walk ten feet seemed forever, but she made it and was just sitting down when she heard a knock at the door. Damon yelled to hang on and he helped her sit back in the chair.

"Now, ten minutes sitting, then I want you to try and stand up. Don't walk anywhere, just stand up. Call one of the nurses to help you up until you can do it without swaying. I'm going to take out the catheter if you can do this for three hours. And I'll let Pi bring you in something to eat tonight. Better?"

"Yes. Much better. Thank you, Damon. I don't…you have been so…I'm sorry."

"Don't be, sweetheart. Listen, I have to talk to you after this is over. It's nothing major, but I need to speak with you about a medical issue. You can talk it over with Jamie if you want him here or not. It affects both of you anyway. I'll be in when the rest leave."

Dane was suddenly afraid and Jamie must have felt it because he wheeled over to her and held her hand. His smile was a forced bright, but she was glad for it. Devin, Cait, and Agent Brownville walked it as Damon went out.

"Hello, dollface," Devin said with a wink. "How's it going? You look a little pale. If you want to put this off for later, I'm sure the agent will understand. He heard your scream of pain so he probably knows you're hurt."

That explains why he's pale, she thought, and shook her head. "No, I'd like to get this over with. I have a new house to see to and I want to set up my practice."

She started off telling him how long she'd known Market, AKA Markus, AKA Lionel, and a host of other names. Yes, she knew him from when she lived in China. No, she didn't know he was charging people tens of thousands of dollars for her help. No, she never charged anyone for anything.

"We think you might know this man." He handed her a picture. "His name is Carl Winchester. He and Market have been friends for about as long as you've know him. He was also acquainted with your mother."

"Yes. Markus told me that he had contacted my mother at some point after I fled to China. You do realize that I was estranged from my mother for a very long time, right?" Dane handed him back the picture and had an overwhelming need to wash her hand.

"Yes. We don't know the whys, of course, but we know you have been in contact with only your maternal grandmother for the past nine and a half years until her recent death. Dr. Wallace, were you aware that Winchester was your uncle? He was your mother's brother."

Shocked, Dane looked over at James. "No. I did...he said that he knew me and that I was a willful child, but I thought he meant from the last time I saw him. He was the one who...he used the whip on me both times."

"We think Market killed him. Of course we'll never know why, but we think it had to do with the...the state in which we found you in. There was no waking you and we think that Market was mad about that. We believe he had been burying the body when the chopper landed to take you here. He was surprised and when he saw you being taken away, he shot at young Grant here. Detective Grant then shot and killed him. She saved two of my men because of her quick thinking."

"I owe her a great deal myself. I don't think I'd be alive if she hadn't contacted my grandmother all those years ago. If she hadn't have intervened, my mother would have had me put away and probably eventually killed. My mother wasn't thrilled to have me as a daughter."

"Can't understand that, you know? Children are the way of the world. Have seven of my own. Well, Dr. Wallace, I don't have anything else unless you want to tell me why Market kidnapped you in the first place. Mr. Grant here, your attorney, told me his theory. Now why don't you tell me yours?"

Dane looked at Devin and at his small nod, she reached into his mind. It was right here in the front for her to see and she took it. But the small little detail that had been bothering her was there too. She burst out laughing.

"Ma'am?" The agent looked perplexed, and she smiled at him.

"I have just inherited a great deal of money and I think he might have heard about it. I had told Markus, or Market, that I was quitting and he may have taken it hard. I was helping him figure out some missing children cases and he assumed I would continue."

"And that's funny to you? I'm sorry, I don't understand." She could see that he didn't. "We know he threatened you about coming to help him, but what made you so important?"

"I think he had it in his head that I was some sort of mind reader, if you can believe that. Some people will believe anything, won't they? Even going so far as to put babies all over someone so that they can have good touches to make them feel better. Isn't that right, Caitlynne?"

"Worked, didn't it?" Cait mumbled. Devin burst out laughing and James was crushing a pillow in his face to hide whatever he was doing. Shaking his head, the agent left.

Cait helped Dane stand up for her ten minutes and they hugged. Careful of the fresh wounds, the women held each other very tightly and cried softly. Devin pulled out his cell phone and snapped a picture.

"No one believes you have a heart down at the station, Cait. This way, I can charge them to see that you do. I bet they still won't believe it, but I can make a quick buck." Laughing, he avoided her slap and reached for her briefcase. "I've been busy, little miss billionaire. I've opened all the accounts in your name and I've had all the utilities switched over to both yours and Jamie's names. I hope that is all right. I have credit cards for you to use and I also went ahead and put Pi's name on one."

"Good, she'll need it. And the other thing, you have it done too?" Dane had called Devin from the mall right before she had been taken.

"Yes. Here, Jamie. It's a pre-nup. It basically says that everything she has is now yours. The house, the money, everything that you purchase as a couple, and everything you purchase separately is now half yours."

Jamie looked at the paper and then at Dane. "You can't do this. This isn't right. This is your money."

"No, it's ours. You take me, you take all of me. Including Pi." She smiled at him. "She's part of the deal too. We are a pair. Can you deal with that?"

"Yes, but this isn't necessary. You could have just said it. There was no need to draw up any kind of paperwork."

"Actually, there is. If anyone ever comes along to contest her grandmother's will, you will be someone else they'll have to argue with. This makes good business sense. And it gives you shared responsibility too. How you two work it out behind closed doors is fine, but this is legal. That's all I have for now. I have some other things we'll need to go over later when you're feeling better. And after you're married, there'll be a few more things, but for now, you're okay."

Devin got up to leave after Jamie signed the document. Cait helped Dane stand again and then she left too. Jamie still looked shocked, but he seemed okay with it. Damon walked in a minute or two later.

"Okay. I called your doctor in China. Dr. Carlton, do you remember him?" She did, but not all that well. "He was out of Beijing. Pi was almost helpful in finding him. She kept calling him 'Cutty-town.' Took me forever to figure it out. Anyway, I called him after you were brought in. He sent me your records." He flopped down on her bed as he spoke.

"He was the doctor that I saw when Nathan and I got married. He did a physical on us both. Mrs. Wallace, Nathan's mother, said it was to make sure I wasn't bringing any diseases to her son."

"Right." Damon grinned. "That's what he said too. Did you ever get in touch with him afterwards or even after the divorce?"

"No. I...we went forward with the wedding, so I figured everything was all right. I didn't see any reason to contact him. Why?" She didn't like his look. He looked like he was going to impart some news, and she was sure she didn't want to hear it.

"Here, read this. It was part of the file he sent over." She took the paper and started reading. It was in Chinese so she didn't read it out loud.

"I don't understand why I would care about how I could adopt now. Nathan and I aren't even married anymore. Why are you doing this?"

"Oh dear. Wrong section." He shifted through the file and handed her another sheet. "I meant to give you this one."

Dane read it and looked up sharply at Damon. "Is this true?" Then she looked at Jamie.

"Yes. He was surprised when he read it in the paper after your very public divorce and had tried to reach you, but you had moved without a forwarding number. He said he mailed you several letters, but I'm thinking maybe your ex-husband waylaid them." Damon smiled at her.

"Honey? What is it? What's it say?" She handed Jamie the paper. It didn't occur to her that he couldn't read it until he said so.

"It says that Nathan is sterile." Dane looked down at the sheet of paper again. "That due to an infection as a child that left him with a very high temperature, his sperm count is zero. He couldn't get me pregnant, not that I couldn't get pregnant. He told me I was sterile. That I couldn't get pregnant. Nathan never told me it was because of him."

Jamie looked confused. She was sure it would come to him soon. And when it did, he hurt himself trying to get up from the chair.

"Then we can have a baby? Our own? That's wonderful news, isn't it?" She smiled at him and nodded her head. Neither of them could move together much, so they held hands and kissed.

"Well, that's not technically true." Damon told him with a laugh. "You see when you came in, they did a battery of tests. I didn't want to take the chance that he shot you up with something and not find out until you were in the operating room. Good thing too. We could keep the more dangerous meds out of your system. Congratulations, you're going to have a baby. I'd say from the size of your uterus, you're about four weeks gone. Gives you a due date the same as Morgan."

"Holy cow, a baby. We're having a baby. We have to get married right away," Jamie said with a smile.

"I'd say so, yes." Damon didn't move, but still looked odd. He still looked like he had something important to say. Or something he wanted Jamie to say.

Jamie sobered quickly. "Holy shit, Mom is going to kill me."

"Oh yeah. That's a definite." Then Damon burst out laughing.

Now Available in the Grant Brothers Series

Coming Soon in the Grant Brothers Series

About the Author

I woke up one morning and decided to give play time to the people in my head who were keeping me awake. Little did I know that they would be so relentless and want their time right now! I wrote for the pure joy of it and to entertain my family and friends. But mostly it was to get more than an hour of sleep without a story playing out. Of course, the more I write, the more they want. So…well, as a result of sleepless days (I work through the night as a gun toting grandma – nope not a vigilantly but an armed security guard) I have lots of stories written.

Hello! My name is Kathi Barton and I'm an author. I have been married to my very best friend Sonny for at times seems several lifetimes – in a good way, honey. And together we have three wonderful children and then the ones we brought into the world - Paul and Dale Barton, Jason and Wendy Barton and Danielle and Ben Conklin. They have given us seven of the greatest treasures on Earth. They don't live at home seven days a week! No, seriously, seven grandchildren – Gavin, Spring, Ben, Trinity, Sarah, Kelly and Kian.

www.ingramcontent.com/pod-product-compliance
Lightning Source LLC
Chambersburg PA
CBHW020616180626
46810CB00007B/2792